Babber Into . _ Heart

Layla Dorine

A Desolate Press Production

Osage, IA 50461

Chapter 1
The Art of Displacement...and other things

Faint stars still twinkled in the pre-dawn sky, the grip of night refusing to loosen its hold over the world. Tucked into the plush depths of an overstuffed leather chair, Bastian cozied up with his e-reader, soaking in the warmth of the large fireplace that dominated the lobby. Constructed of river rock, it brought the beauty of nature to an already beautiful room, and Bastian rather enjoyed having it all to himself. Honestly, it was the grandest lodge he'd ever stayed at, not that he'd stayed at many, but this was by far the fanciest of them, which was why he felt a little like a fish out of water. It was giving him a bit of imposter syndrome, but his best friend hadn't gotten it when he'd told him that. Of course, he hadn't. This was Chauncy's kind of place and while the two of them really were from different worlds, what they'd bonded over was way more prevalent than the wealth and resources Bastian didn't possess.

People liked to speculate that it was bad, traumatic even. In their minds why else would a boy from Eastman Park with an Ivy League education spend his free time with a kid from the burned out side of the railroad tracks, whose only brush with higher education was the dos and don'ts of the streets.

Truth was, their bond had come from a moment of triumph, stuck in an elevator during a blackout with a pregnant woman whose water had decided to break. They'd worked with her to bring Bastian Chauncy Medlow into the world beside Blake Mathias Medlow, each of the twins wrapped in their shirts when the firemen arrived.

What a contrast that had been. A twenty-dollar rock band t-shirt next to hundred-dollar Armani, and yet Chauncy had taken his off with the same disregard for what might become of it as Bastian had and they'd been fast friends ever since. In the elevator, they'd shared childhood stories in the hopes of entertaining the first time mom, who was nervous, worried, and desperate to breathe and laugh through the pain. By the time they'd been freed and guided out into a Washington State evening, they were tired, hungry, and more than ready for ice coffee and pizza: supreme, no black olives with extra soft mozzarella cheese melting in puddles all over that pie.

That had made them laugh too, especially when their coffee order had proved to be another similarity. Bastian hadn't laughed so much since Shep, his best friend since elementary school, had gone off to pursue work in California. After that, they'd bumped into each other everywhere, until they started making a point to get together, which had somehow led to joining the same kink club along with the same gym. They'd started doubling up at the club while they learned what they loved and what they had little interest in, which was how they'd ended up here. There was a month long series of training sessions culminating in a pet play event and somehow, probably between shots of tequila, Bastian had let himself be talked into signing up.

Bastian still didn't know how he felt about these upcoming sessions, but he knew shy Chauncy wasn't going to come to the event until he'd agreed to come too.

So now here he was, sky streaked with the brilliant colors of dawn. There was enough light to see by, at least for what he wanted to do. He closed the cover on his e-reader and slipped it in his backpack beside a spare t-shirt, zipped it up, and left it with the front desk receptionist before heading out. The moment he reached the path, he broke into a jog. Walking it yesterday had shown him where the obstacles were: benches, low hanging limbs, short retaining walls, planters, and waist high shrubs. Those he could practice doing summersaults over.

There was a freedom and exhilaration in flipping and bouncing off things, in twisting and making his body spiral. He loved gymnastics, but this was different; this was parkour, free running, also known as the art of displacement, and he was damned good at it. Breathing rhythmically, he exhaled as he leapt on the back of a bench, paused for a heartbeat, then spun, hurling himself through the air until his feet hit the grass and he was off running again. It wasn't about speed, it wasn't about keeping time, it was about the effortlessness of it all.

As he neared the end of the trail, he debated making a second run, but the sun was fully up over the horizon and people were starting to move about. Already he'd had to retime a jump to avoid crashing into a fellow jogger, and the looks he was getting? Well, he wasn't in the mood to explain what it was he was doing. Hell, he wasn't quite ready for any human interaction at all, especially not with a stranger.

Chauncy was supposed to be the shy one, not him. They were so screwed.

His stomach growled, which was the last bit of encouragement he needed to head in. If he knew his friend, Chauncy would only just be contemplating getting out of bed. He'd have the television on, phone in hand as he scrolled the internet, checked emails and bullshitting with members of his circle on social media. Depending on the stories from the night before and the number of photos accompanying them, he'd be at it for a while, meaning Bastian would have plenty of time to stand beneath the pounding rhythm of the shower spray in their bathroom, mentally preparing himself for the first training session later that afternoon.

Training.

What the fuck had he gotten himself into?

All the way back to the room he tried not to imagine what the day had in store for him, but vivid images kept rolling through his mind, each more horrifying than the one before. He wished he had more experience with this, then maybe he'd have a better idea of what to expect.

Oh, Bastian had wanted to. He'd thought about it, wondered what it would feel like to be under the hands of a gentle trainer who'd stroke his furred sides, rub noses with him and know just how to help him settle into pet space. It was why they were here a month before the adoption event was set to start, to train and learn as much as they could in the hopes that they might be adopted. Only Bastian knew in the back of his head that only Chauncy had the chance to make that happen. Try as he might, Bastian had never seen himself as true pet material. Pets aimed to please. They were soft, adorable, happy little submissives that prided themselves on being the best they could be for their masters.

Bastian didn't want to be owned, he wanted to be kept, which, in his head at least, was something entirely different.

If only he could properly put it into words and explain it, then maybe he might stand a chance of conveying it to someone else. What he did know was that at heart, he was a ferret. He'd always admired the clever, cunning, nimble little animals, their behaviors reminding him a great deal of the parkour he loved. Watching them run through tubes and up and down the ramps of their cages always brought him a great deal of joy, and in his head, he could picture himself that way, which was why he'd spared no expense to find himself the most realistic ferret costume that he could manage.

He loved the feel of a hand stroking his head or dancing down his arm, but it was hard for him to stay still for that for long. The truth was he loved playing more and the club he and Chauncy belonged to had one of the coolest play spaces he'd ever seen. There were tubes to crawl in and out of, flip over and sprawl on top of, and soft mats where he could summersault and even manage the occasional handstand. Okay, so maybe he was a little bit of a showoff, bringing his parkour into his playtime in a way that tended to send others scurrying out of his way.

It had gained him a lot of looks and a great deal of attention. Those who'd ventured close had always been eager to get him to settle down and sit beside them, which had always led to too much squirming on his part. He never quite knew how to convey to them that as long as he was moving, engaging in something physical, his mind was in that beautiful space where he needed it to be. When he was expected to be still, when it felt, even in the slightest, like they were trying to change or control him, he wanted nothing more than to be as far away from them as he could get.

He was gonna fail as a pet, despite the month of training he was about to subject himself to, and that was enough to leave him feeling a bit melancholy and apprehensive as he entered his hotel room.

"Did you have a good run?" Chauncy asked as soon as he'd gotten the door closed. Sure enough, Chauncy was exactly where he figured, with the television on some early morning talk show and his phone in his hand.

"Remind me again why coming here was a good idea?"

"You mean aside from the intensive training sessions and the opportunity to explore something we've been talking about for years?"

"Okay, there is that, but…I don't know, at least at the club, we know the people there."

"And have either of us been lucky enough to find a good master yet?"

"I don't want a master," Bastian growled, bristling as soon as he heard the word.

"I know, I know, I shouldn't have said it. I knew you were going to get testy as soon as the word slipped out of my mouth."

"Sorry, I just…"

"I get it, okay, I do. Even if I think it's splitting hairs at this point. All I was trying to point out was that here, we'd have the chance to meet people who were actively looking for pets. We'd have the best opportunity to get to know them and show them what potentially amazing pets we could be."

"Yeah, I know. I guess I'm still having a hard time feeling like I belong here. I'm not…"

Gesturing between himself and Chauncy, he tried to find words to convey what he was feeling without worrying about accidentally offending his friend. That was the last thing he wanted to do.

"Soft, meek, mild mannered? In a word, me?" Chauncy replied, the slightest change to his tone conveying that Bastian had failed in his desire not to hit a nerve. Best to unruffle those feathers before they grew into pouting and those sad eyed looks that always made Bastian scramble to do whatever he could think of to make them go away. Including subject himself to another of Chauncy's poorly thought-out schemes. The last one had landed him at a combination speed dating/wine and fondue party. Whoever had thought to put those things together had either been a genius or consumed so many bottles of whiskey that anything would have seemed like a good idea to them.

Bastian had found himself bored to tears listening to one guy spend the entire five minutes talking about the latest account his firm had landed. He had gotten a good laugh when the guy he'd crashed into thanks to an errant flip early that morning, had plunked down at the table still sporting the bruised cheek Bastian had accidently given him. There had been an almost moment there, when it seemed like they'd connected, then the man had started rambling on about a conspiracy theorist he admired. Bastian had been relieved when the buzzer had gone off. He might not keep up with the news as much as Chauncy did, but he preferred it to consist of facts, rather than fervently defended fiction.

"You know that's not what I meant," Bastian said, leaning against the wall beside the television set.

"What I know is that you're terrified of letting your guard down again so you're trying really hard to convince yourself that you don't want the same things I do," Chauncy said, tossing the phone beside him on the bed and giving

Bastian his undivided attention. "Everyone you meet isn't going to be another Claude."

The mere mention of his ex's name sent a shudder of revulsion down Bastian's spine, his nose wrinkled, and he shifted his weight to lean a little harder against the wall, seeking support and a hint of comfort from it. It wasn't as soft and comforting as the press of strong arms holding him close, but it was far easier on his nerves.

"See, that right there proves my point entirely."

Straightening up, Bastian attempted to frown at him and found he didn't have the energy. "What?"

"You know what."

The fierceness in his friend's gaze was a reminder that Bastian might try to fool himself, but he wasn't going to pull anything over on Chauncy. It was part of why they got along so well together. Even when Bastian was trying to hide his innermost feelings, Chauncy always managed to suss them out and get him to confront them.

"I wouldn't call it terrified, more like pessimistically cautious," Bastian grumbled, shuffling from one foot to the next. "I just...I put up with Claude's shit way longer than I've ever tolerated anyone's crap, and I still can't figure out why. Maybe if I understood that part, I could trust that I wouldn't fuck up so spectacularly again."

"First off, let's get one thing straight. You didn't fuck up. You were you. He was the one who wanted to change you into a compliant little kitten who hung on his every word. I hardly recognized you when you were around him. Before he came along, I'd never known you to let someone speak for you or cajole you into doing something you didn't want to do."

Bastian cocked an eyebrow at his friend before gesturing around the room at the two queen beds and the desk in the corner. "And what do you call this?"

"Helping you be exactly where you'd like to be."

"You sure sound certain of that."

"Because I know you, Bas, and you wouldn't have come if you really didn't want to. You'd have told me to fuck right the hell off, and that would have been that, but you didn't. You got in the car and even took charge of the radio, which is always a sign that you're in a good mood. Especially when you land on the alternative station."

"What's my choice in radio stations have to do with anything?"

Chauncy studied him for a moment, then shook his head. "You really don't know, do you?"

"If I did, I wouldn't have asked the question."

"Fair enough. It's just that when you're pissed, you always go for the metal station, when you're sad, it's always country, and when you're feeling mellow, it's classic rock. Alternative is for when you're pleased about something, even when you refuse to admit it."

With a groan, Bastian slid down the wall to sit on the floor in front of it. "Okay so maybe there *is* some truth to what you're saying. I wanted out of the city and there's no denying that it's beautiful up here. The pictures I saw online didn't do it justice. I'm dying to take a canoe out and go paddling around the lake."

"Just don't fall in."

"Wow, I would never have thought of that myself."

"Ha. Ha."

Heaving a sigh, Bastian ran his fingers through his sweaty hair and tugged a little. The slight scratching of his nails along his scalp and the gentle tugging helped ground him enough to find the words he'd been reluctant to say. "What if I'm wrong and I'm not meant to be a pet?"

"Haven't you told me over and over how much you enjoy your ferret head space and how free it makes you feel?"

"Yeah, but…"

"No buts. You are a pet, end of story and what you need is a Master who's willing to take the time to explore what you need from him, and what you can give him in return. As far as I'm concerned, you jumped into things far too quickly with Claude, and you allowed his words to speak louder than his actions. Just because someone says they're a Master doesn't mean they truly know what it means to be one, and if, by chance, they do, it still doesn't mean they'll be the right Master for you."

"How come you know so much more than I do when we started down this road together?"

"Maybe because I *am* too scared and shy to take a chance on anyone until I am one million percent positive they are going to be the right one," Chauncy admitted. "I don't know if I'd have the courage to pick myself up and try again if things went wrong and I lost a Daddy I'd come to love."

"I never loved Claude."

"Good."

"But I wanted to."

"Of course you did."

"Do you have to say it like that?"

"Like what?"

"All sarcastic and shit."

"In this case, yeah, because there was no way in hell you were ever going to fall in love with that fussy, pretentious flake, and you only hurt yourself by trying. He wasn't worth the time you wasted on him."

"Amen to that."

"I think you were just enthralled by the chance to play rather than sit on the sidelines and watch."

Chauncy paused for a moment, like he wanted to be certain his words were getting through to Bastian, whose shoulders and neck were beginning to feel tense as another wave of anxiety rolled over him.

"Can I tell you something?" Chauncy asked, breaking the silence that had filled the room.

"Always."

"Despite knowing what a shithead Claude was, I was jealous of what you had with him."

Chauncy's words caught him so off guard that Bastian snorted and sat gaping at him until he was reminded that for all his talk, Chauncy had never even made it onto the playroom floor, let alone taken part in full on sessions the way Bastian had. "It wasn't worth being jealous of."

"Then don't you think you deserve something that is?"

"No. I think we both do."

Chapter 2
It's all about being safe and being you

Shimmers of early morning sunlight made the man's hair sparkle with shades of gold and red. Jarrod could only imagine what its true color really was. Honey, maybe, or perhaps caramel? Maybe it leaned closer to bronze, or even auburn, or it could be that he was completely off base, and it was some mix of ruby and berry, striking and rich enough to eclipse the glory of the rising sun. Pressing his fingers to the glass, Jarrod leaned against the window, enraptured by the fluid movements of the man below. He'd seen parkour before, in videos and the occasional TV show, but never like this. Never right beneath his nose.

With a graceful mix of power and agility, the man launched himself off the back of a bench, executed a sort of corkscrew summersault and landed with the ease of a cat. There was barely a moment of pause before he took off running again, diving over a shrub to tuck and roll on the other side. Ten pushups later he was dashing down the empty path, fading from Jarrod's view all too rapidly when the tree lined trail curved north.

What a fine ass that was moving beneath those sweatpants. Jarrod leaned until his nose was pressed to the *glass, straining for even a hint of another view. No way it wasn't as firm as it looked. Taking himself in hand, he imagined the feel of it beneath his fingers, taunt, tight…*

"Jarrod. Hey! Did you hear anything I said?"

Blinking, Jarrod stared across the table at Lance and tried to recall the last thing his friend had said to him, but his thoughts kept drifting back to the man doing parkour on the trail that morning and how much he longed to see him in action again.

"Dude, you've been staring at that spinner of jelly containers for the last five minutes. Considering there are only four flavors, and you hate marmalade, it shouldn't be that difficult of a choice."

"Sorry, guess I'm just distracted this morning."

"No shit. Care to share, or shall I attempt to guess what's got you staring at those packets like the secrets of the universe are written down their sides?"

"You are not as funny as you think you are."

"Are you so sure about that?"

"Meh."

"Seriously though, you might want to think about eating your breakfast before it gets colder than I'm sure it already is."

"Who said I didn't like it this way?"

Lance threw up his hands, shook his head and turned his attention back to the quarter of a pancake he still had left. Because he was feeling a tad bit prickly, Jarrod slathered marmalade on one slice of toast and apple jelly on the other, just to prove to Lance that he wasn't always right about everything. Of course, the grin on Lance's face when Jarrod grimaced at the first taste of orange was a sure sign that he hadn't accomplished shit besides screwing up his own meal, which was as cold and unappealing as Lance suggested it would be, damn it all.

Several bites in, he sipped his coffee only to discover that it too was at less-than-optimal temperature. Ice coffee had never been his thing, but he drank it anyway, if only to avoid giving Lance the satisfaction of saying *I told you so*.

"Seriously though, I don't mean to give you shit. I know your first training session starts in a few hours. You're probably trying to focus on the lesson you're going to teach, while I'm over here babbling on and on about the rising cost of eggs and bacon."

"You're not wrong. Going to the grocery store is like volunteering to become a robbery victim. You might as well eat the cash for all the good it does."

"No thanks, I'm not a fan of green leafy substances as it is. I don't want to eat anything that tastes like dirty paper and other people's germs."

"A little garlic powder, some salt and pepper, and you never know."

"I know enough to just buy the groceries, damn."

Snickering, Jarrod was finally able to focus on finishing the rest of his food, though the image of the twisting, flipping man was firmly entrenched in his mind. Out of the corner of his eye, he caught the barest glint of something reddish-gold and turned his head for a closer look, but the woman conversing with animated gestures was too tall and curvy to be the man he'd watched so intently.

"Glad to see I'm boring the fuck out of you this morning."

There was humor in Lance's voice, coupled with a touch of annoyance.

When Jarred glanced back at him, he saw Lance looking in the woman's direction, eyeing her up and down. "Though I gotta admit, if you're gonna be distracted, that isn't a bad way to go about it."

"Unfortunately for me, she isn't the person I want to be distracted by."

"Is that you saying there *is* a person like that running around?"

"Could be."

"Dude, the very least you could do is share after how utterly rude you've been this morning. I mean, damn, if I had thinner skin I might actually be offended."

Jarrod paused, newly refilled coffee cup halfway to his lips, and raised an eyebrow at him. "Fortunately, your ego can take a bruising, considering how much of it there is."

"Ha. Ha. Ha."

Silence descended over the table for several minutes, while Jarrod finished his utterly unappealing meal, and Lance ogled a few of the folks that passed through the room. His friend's tastes had a way of changing like the ocean tide, whereas Jarrod's, well, his thoughts drifted back to the parkour running man. While Jarrod didn't think he had a type, the guy had certainly piqued his interest. Without meeting him, it was impossible to know if there was anything to him that would hold it, but for now, Jarrod could dream.

"Yeah, and on that note, I'm gonna get going before I get a complex over here."

Sighing heavily, Jarrod dialed his focus back in on Lance, who'd already risen half out of his seat. "Sorry 'bout that."

"Don't be sorry, just dish the deets later when you have the time."

"Long as you do the same."

"Huh? What do you mean? I'm not the one distracted by a phantom someone."

"Neither am I. He is very real, even if I haven't had the privilege of meeting him yet," Jarrod admitted. "The details I'm looking for from you are about your session."

"Sounds like a fair enough trade to me."

"Good deal. Are you sure you're ready for this?"

"As ready as I'll ever be."

"Just…remember what we talked about. You want to learn, but you don't want to lose yourself in the process. Each pet is meant to be special and unique. The training should be more about helping you become your best self than molding you into a cookie-cutter version of someone else's ideal pet."

"I won't forget."

"Good, have fun. I can't wait to hear all about it later."

"Same."

With a small wave, Lance headed on his way, while Jarrod took a moment to gather his thoughts before heading for the lodge gym. As always, lifting had a sort of meditative feel for him. He never counted the reps, he just listened to the steady clang and let his thoughts wander until his mind was silent and calm. It was in the silence that his first lesson came to him, not that he hadn't had a list of the ones he wanted to teach, just that the jumping off point hadn't solidified itself in his mind until now.

He worked his arms and shoulders until he'd made three cycles through each machine. Sweat poured down his body when he was done. It was definitely time for a shower and maybe a bit of relaxing before it was time to teach. As the returning pony master, he'd taken what he'd done last year and looked to improve upon it, researching and attending sessions to learn all he could before coming back this year. As far as he was concerned, it was up to him to ensure that each of the ponies had the best experience possible, and the best chance at getting chosen on adoption day.

It had pleased him greatly to see how many had found their Masters last year. Several had written to him over the past twelve months to tell him how things were going in their relationships. They'd thanked him for being an ear for them when they had questions they worried about posing to their new Daddies, especially in relationships where distance was an issue and insecurities arose. That was something he planned to address this year before turning his ponies back out into the world. They needed to know how to navigate entering those kinds of relationships, what to ask for, what to expect, what questions to pose and how to lay out their concerns before they festered into issues. For today though, he just wanted to get to know them.

It was with that thought firmly in mind that he showered, soaked up some sun via the window in his room, dressed, and headed down to prepare for his first pony training session. According to the roster, he had seven ponies signed up this year. It was nice to not be overloaded, it would allow him the opportunity to get to know each one better, and suss out how best to help them grow and thrive.

As he always did, he arrived early, greeting each of the men as they entered the room. It turned out that there were eight of them, one having managed to get in just under the wire.

The room had no chairs. Instead, he'd rolled out several thick purple and black gymnastics mats for his ponies to get comfortable on. There was three feet of space between each one. He'd arranged them in a horseshoe shape to create a more intimate atmosphere. No one was seated so far away that he'd need to raise his voice to be heard.

"Alright everyone," Jarrod said with a clap of his hands. "Find a seat and get comfortable. Today isn't about playing, we'll get to that soon enough, I promise you. Before I can expect to teach you anything, though, I need to get to know you and talk to you a little about what you expect to get out of these training sessions. Once we start rolling, things will get intense. I want to make sure each of you is prepared for that."

"How are we supposed to be prepared when we have no idea what you have in store for us?" a blond in a gray t-shirt asked.

"Thomas, right?"

"I umm, prefer Tommy if that's okay?"

"It's perfectly alright with me, Tommy. The key is for you to be comfortable here. That goes for all of you. I want you to feel free to ask any question that comes to mind and stop me anytime you want further clarification on something or simply don't understand what I'm asking of you."

He waited for them to nod in understanding before plunging into the lesson.

"Now, to answer Tommy's question, being prepared for this class requires only one thing. Showing up relaxed and eager to learn. That's all. I want each of you to leave any and all preconceived notions about what a pony is supposed to be at the door of the room before you come in. The truth is that not all ponies like to wear bits. Not all ponies like to pull carriages. Some ponies love a tail that attaches while others want a tail with a plug on the other end. Some ponies wear the full hood while others don't like things over their faces. Some wear headbands, some love to practice dressage, some don't mind a harness, some hate to be struck by a whip. The thing I want you each to understand is that you will define the type of pony you want to be, otherwise, you can find yourself pulled out of your headspace due to discomfort and even stress."

"Isn't the point supposed to be that it's not stressful?" a man with waist length black hair asked. "We're supposed to be turning over all control to our handler. Once the reins are in their hands, all the stress, and everything else we don't want to deal with is supposed to melt away."

"Yes and no," Jarrod replied. "That's the goal but let me ask you this. If every time you moved there was something jabbing you in the side or squeezing your ribs, would you want to pull a cart or follow any direction you'd been given?"

Midnight hair, who Jarrod was almost certain was named Frost, emphatically shook his head.

"And if something was jabbing at you and making you feel uncomfortable, you wouldn't be able to lose yourself in your role, right?"

"No, I'd be too busy trying to figure out what it was and how to make it stop."

"Exactly, so tell me something, Frost, how can you expect to give yourself over to another and let them guide you if you're feeling uncomfortable in your own skin?"

"I…I don't know. I guess I wouldn't be able to."

"Exactly," Jarrod said, then looked around at the other ponies in the room. "How many of you have worn a saddle and been ridden?"

Only one pony, one of the largest of the men in the room, raised his hand. For the life of him, Jarrod couldn't remember his name.

"Was the person who was riding you smaller in size?"

"Oh yes, my old mistress was tiny."

"She would have had to be, to not hurt you," Jarrod said. "The human back wasn't meant to be sat on for long periods of time, especially not by an adult. There are saddles and there are many who wear them and carry their riders that way, but in order for it to be comfortable, there has to be a balance, either in size or in the way the pony is ridden."

"You mean like side saddle versus astride?" Tommy asked.

"Not exactly," Jarrod said. "Having someone try to ride you side saddle wouldn't be very comfortable at all. It would put all their weight to one side of you and make it harder for you to move. What I was referring to was the practice of riding with the rider supporting most of their own weight so they weren't sitting fully on you."

"Ohh."

"Think of it this way," Jarrod began. "I'm a muscular guy. I'm not a featherweight. While I might not be taller than you, I suspect I am heavier than you are by at least twenty pounds. If I were to saddle you up and sit fully on your back, it would be rather difficult and uncomfortable for you to carry me around the room. We've already established that being uncomfortable would keep you from achieving the desired headspace, so it wouldn't be a positive experience for you, now would it?"

"No, Sir."

"But, you're a pony, right? So if he, I'm sorry, I don't remember your name," Jarrod said while pointing to the big guy.

"Greg."

"Yes, thank you. I won't forget again," Jarrod assured him. "Greg was ridden. So, by that assumption, if he could carry someone around the room, shouldn't I assume you can too?"

Tommy shook his head.

"Why not?"

Tommy licked his lips and looked around him at the other members of the training session, understanding dawning in his eyes. "Because we're all different. Greg being ridden doesn't mean that I can be too, even by someone the same size as the person who rode him. I'm not as big as he is. Even a small rider might be hard to carry for anything except a very short distance, and trying to carry someone of your size would just leave me with a backache."

"And if you are in pain…" Jarrod prodded.

"I can't be a good pony."

"Exactly," Jarrod said. "This is why you have to explore what aspects of pony play will work for you, as well as what will not. I don't want any of you to come here thinking that you need to perform the way you've seen others perform, or the way you've read about in some online article. I'm not saying there's anything wrong with them, there isn't, just that the only way to learn what's right for you is to experience different aspects and be honest with yourself, your trainers and your handlers. There's nothing to be gained from trying to force yourself to endure something because someone else thinks you should, is that understood?"

Jarrod waited for his words to sink in, and only when they all nodded did he continue on.

"In this room, I want you to find the headspace you desire. To do that, you need to first touch base with your inner pony and help it come out," Jarrod said. "Now, I want each of you to close your eyes, and do some simple, rhythmic breathing. In through the nose, out through the mouth. Let your shoulders relax, let your body curve forward if it's more comfortable. Don't focus on breathing, don't try and count the breaths, instead, I want you to look inward and picture your pony self."

Jarrod fell silent for a little bit, letting them settle in and do as they were told. "Maybe you're whickering softly, waiting to have your face and ears rubbed. Maybe you're all harnessed up, waiting to pull your handler's carriage in a Pride parade. Maybe you've got a loose harness on, something that is tethering you, but not constricting. Perhaps you like it tight, hugging you and keeping you safe. Is your tail tickling the back of your thighs? Do your ears bob as you move, or do they stand up straight and proud? Are you performing? Turning around a show ring and making your handler proud? In your mind's eye, picture what your role looks like and what you want to get out of the headspace you're entering into."

He gave them the time to do as he asked, watching to see who fidgeted and who seemed to sink into the exercise. Most seemed steady and sure, but two, Ryan and Frost, rubbed their hands along their thighs, rocked, or pressed their fingers together. Sometimes they scrunched up their noses, like they were trying too hard to picture themselves. With those actions, he could see that their level of inexperience was even greater than the rest. No worries though, it was his job to ensure they learned. All this exercise did was help him see who might need a little more help.

"Before you come to each session, I want you to revisit this exercise and enter the room focused on your inner pony. That's the only pony that should matter to you moving forward, and that is the one you'll want to find a handler for."

Chapter 3
When understanding is sought and found

Bastian left the first training session for miscellaneous pets a little unsettled. He'd gone in expecting to be told all the things that would be expected of him as a pet but left with a great deal of things to think about. His trainer, Daddy William, had asked them all why they associated themselves with the creatures they envisioned themselves to be. Down the row he'd gone, patiently awaiting each of their answers.

When Bastian had hesitantly stumbled over his explanation of his ferret tendencies, Daddy William had helped draw the words out of him by asking what characteristics he shared with the diminutive creatures. When Bastian explained his love of parkour, and the rambunctious way he loved to roll and tumble about a playroom, Daddy William had said that being a ferret seemed like the perfect fit for him.

He hadn't been bothered in the slightest when Bastian said he needed to play hard before he could settle down, he'd just asked if safety had ever been a factor and if that was something he hoped a Daddy could help him with. When he'd replied with "*if they want*", Daddy William had shaken his head, booped him gently on the nose and said, *"no, it's if you want"*.

When Daddy William had gone on to tell each of them the type of Daddy they gave the impression that they each needed, Bastian had been shocked to his very core at how on target he was. A little bit humbled too, since Chauncy had been attempting to tell him the same thing, and he'd stubbornly refused to hear his friend.

He'd apologize tonight, over dinner, while the two were comparing notes from their sessions. Chauncy's would start in about an hour when the kittens gathered in the room Bastian had just left.

Know who you are, be who you are, and know what you need, Daddy William had told them all before they left the room, reinforcing what Bastian had already known. Claude hadn't been the right Daddy for him, in fact, after just one session with Daddy William, Bastian was no longer certain if Claude was a proper Daddy at all, not when Daddy William had spoken at length about what a Daddy was supposed to offer their pets.

Among those things had been safety, security, and the freedom to be who they were meant to be. That last part truly stood out for him, and he told himself, with all certainty, that the next time he accepted a Daddy into his life, he was only going to do so once he was certain those needs were met. Scrolling through his phone as he headed back into the crisp outdoors, he decided to take a stroll down by the water while he tried to sort out what to order in for their evening meal.

Talk about overwhelming. There were way too many restaurants to sort out, so he decided to search by category and hope something in the pictures sparked an interest. Wings, burgers, pizza, meh, he wasn't in the mood for any of them. He'd just scrolled again when he slammed into something solid enough to send him reeling backward. Only a firm grip on his arm kept him from hitting the ground.

Blinking, Bastian stared into intense eyes alight with worry and a hint of amusement.

"Might want to glance up from time to time," a deep voice rumbled. "If you keep on the path you're going you're libel to wind up inadvertently wading in the lake, which isn't the warmest this time of year."

Snickering, Bastian couldn't help but be reminded of Chauncy's earlier comment to him, warning him to be careful if he should go canoeing, least he wind up sinking or overturning himself. As distracted as he'd been lately, he wasn't wrong.

A couple inches shorter than him, but packing way more mass, all in the form of muscle, the man had a powerful look about him, but his gaze, rather than being hard and overly serious like so many others Bastian had seen wandering around the hotel, was lively and filled with amusement. His smile was one Bastian wouldn't have minded looking at longer, only he was suddenly quite aware of the fact that he was staring. He hadn't even apologized for carelessly crashing into the man.

"Sorry about slamming into you," Bastian said, lowering his gaze as the man slowly released his hold on him.

"I'm not," the man replied. It seemed like he had more to say only Bastian heard his name bellowed across the lawn and turned just in time to see a frantic Chauncy rushing toward him, huffing, puffing and clearly short of breath.

"Can you…let me….into our…room," Chauncy gasped when he reached Bastian's side. "I forgot my wallet on the end table."

"Again," Bastian said, slinging an arm around his friend's shoulder. "Come on, let's get you reunited with it, and maybe the next time I suggest getting a chain so you can keep it tethered, you won't scoff at the suggestion."

"I scoff because a chain and slacks simply don't go together. Talk about a fashion faux pas," Chauncy grumbled, waving at the air in front of him like he was trying to shoo the very thought out of existence.

"You know how to fix that, right?" Bastian said, unbothered by his friend's antics.

"No."

"Start wearing jeans."

Chauncy's laughter rung out over the lawn as Bastian turned to glance back at the man he'd crashed into. "Thanks for sparing me a dip in the lake," he called over his shoulder. "In the future I'll do a better job of watching where I'm going."

"Not on account of me, I hope," the man replied, leaving Bastian to wonder what he meant as Chauncy whisked him away.

"I am so sorry. I know this is the second time in two days that I've left it upstairs," Chauncy babbled breathlessly. "I was in a rush to grab lunch so I could take my meds, then I went into town for a few things, only to realize, at the damned cash register, that I'd left my wallet behind. I asked them to just leave everything in the cart, and I hope they listened, because I don't have the time to wander through the place again, but oh my god, when you see my finds, you'll get it."

No, he really wouldn't. Half the time he wasn't sure what the hell it was his friend was showing him. Chauncy had a love of antiquing that he'd been trying to pass on to Bastian for years, but in all that time, he still hadn't been able to grasp why being old seemed to translate into being expensive.

"I'm going to order in dinner," Bastian said as they walked. "Any idea what you might want?"

"Not pizza."

"Yeah, I wasn't in the mood for that either, or burgers, or wings."

"Or subs."

"Ugg, after the ones we got on the way up here I might never be in the mood for subs again."

"Don't remind me. I'm still having nightmares about that mystery meat. If there is one thing that I'm absolutely certain of, it's that it wasn't chicken."

"Told you not to eat it."

"You ate yours."

"No, I ate less than half of mine, decided that finishing it would have been akin to gastrological torture, and pitched the rest when we stopped for gas, remember?"

"Not particularly, I was busy running inside to puke."

"True," Bas replied. "Thank you by the way."

"For what?"

"Not doing it in the car."

"It was damned close, let me tell you."

"I bet it was."

A blast of cool air hit them when they stepped into their hotel room. It had been a pleasant thing to discover that neither of them could sleep if a room was too warm. Others might call it freezing, but for him and Chauncy, it was crisp and comfortable, much like early mornings outside of the hotel. While Bas plopped down on the edge of his bed, Chauncy rushed for his wallet, checked that he had his room key, and hurried for the door.

"How's Himalayan sound?" Bastian called after him.

"Interesting! Go for it."

The sound of the door shutting punctuated his friend's words, leaving Bastian to sprawl on his back and study the menu, or at least, that was what he was supposed to be doing. Three rows in his mind started wandering back to the man who'd saved him from falling on his ass. With arms as powerful as those, he'd probably be able to catch someone in mid-jump or spin, and with a smile like the one he'd flashed, laugh while he was doing it.

His thoughts drifted from the man to Daddy William's words when he'd suggested that Bastian needed a fun loving, playful Daddy who wouldn't try to reign him in but would make sure he stayed safe in the environment he was playing in. That way he could enjoy himself to his fullest without being constrained.

Bastian found himself daydreaming of the types of hugs arms like that could give. Secure ones, tight and all enveloping. The kind that would leave him feeling safe. But were they also the type that would seek to imprison him?

Shaking off his sudden infatuation with those arms, Bastian forced his attention back on the menu, deciding on the Chicken Pakora, Chicken Mo Mo, Sagg Paneer and Lamb Tikka Masala. He got them some Garlic Naan too, and what meal would be complete without a little dessert, especially one meant to be served cold, so he got two orders of Kheer and some mango chutney. Satisfied that they would not only have enough for dinner but some leftover for a little midnight snack if they happened to be up again tonight, he gave in to the urge to daydream again.

At least this time it was about the course he planned to run in the morning. The long row of hedges that lined one section of the trail had been calling to him ever since he laid his eyes on them. Tomorrow morning, the moment there was enough light so he wouldn't crash into one when he tried to leap it, he was going to see how many ways he could flip, dive, or tuck and roll over top of one. There seemed to be enough distance between them to generate speed for the next launch, as long as he timed things accurately. A mistime would mean crashing headlong into a prickly tangle of branches, not that it hadn't happened before. Bastian knew from experience that it would happen again too, though he knew better than to risk serious injury and cause himself to miss any of the training sessions laid out in the upcoming weeks. Especially when he still had projects to complete for his clients. Chauncy might be able to afford to take a month off, but Bastian couldn't put his business on hold for that long. A working vacation was the best he'd been able to manage, and he was grateful for it.

As it was, he felt himself growing more and more excited to see what session two might bring, considering Daddy William truly seemed to understand that Bastian would only be able to settle in and enjoy the cuddles, snuggles and pets that also came with playtime if he'd been allowed to exhaust himself first.

"It just means playtime is your way of getting into the right headspace," Daddy William had suggested. *"No worries, you're not the only pet built that way. Everyone's got to figure out what's right for them. Sounds to me like you're well ahead of the pack, you already know. Just let me*

ask you one thing: Is that something you're wanting as part of your playtime, to end it in someone's arms?"

While the voice in the back of his head screamed an emphatic and enthusiastic yes, Bastian had bitten his bottom lip and been reluctant to answer.

"Let me guess, you do, but you don't want to be seen as needy," Daddy William supplied. "Or am I wrong and you want it but are afraid you won't be let go when you're ready to play again? Did someone cut your playtime short one too many times? Did they pull you out of your headspace by clinging to you and making you feel uncomfortable?"

How had he determined all of that from silence and the smallest of gestures? Words still wouldn't come, he was so shocked at being read so easily, but he nodded, and leaned into the touch when Daddy William ran a gentle hand over the top of his head.

"It isn't needy to want affection, it only becomes a problem when you have no boundaries and refuse to wait, or want it all the time, no matter what your Daddy happens to be doing, though something tells me that'll never be an issue with you, little one. You strike me as the sort to sit in the background and wait until it's offered, even when you've been itching for it. The key is to find you a Daddy who'll give *you what you need without you having to ask for it, or worse, beg."*

It was like he'd been able to see into Bastian's soul and knew that anytime he'd needed something from Claude he'd practically been made to beg for it, punishment for not being the type of pet that Claude could bend to his will. Toxic and passive aggressive, that's what Claude had been. Bastian had seen it clearly early in the relationship, and yet he'd still stuck with him, knowing people like that didn't change. No, they expected everyone else to change for them, and while Bastian had considered it, and even made a few small concessions in his behavior, it had left him chafing to throw off those expectations and go back to being himself. In the end, that's exactly what he had done, only now he was hesitant to let others see him, for fear that they, too would want him to change.

He was gonna be a bad pet.

As much as he tried not to give into that way of thinking, the thought was always there in the back of his mind.

Damn but he wished the food would hurry up. Realistically he knew it was much too soon, he'd only just ordered it, but he needed a distraction from the dark thoughts that wouldn't stop crowding his head. Scrubbing his hands over his face, he attempted to rub them away. When that failed, he conjured up the image of hedges and the possibilities they offered, but before he could picture more than a diving roll, his thoughts shifted again, back to the man he'd crashed into on the path and the strength Bastian had felt coursing through him. He'd hit brick walls that had felt less solid than that.

What had the man said to him, about not paying attention on his account? Did that mean he hadn't minded Bastian crashing into him? If Chauncy hadn't come running along, would he have introduced himself, maybe even struck up a conversation, or was Bastian just reading too much into a few simple words?

The man's smile had been intriguing though, playful and welcoming. It reminded him of something else Daddy William had gotten him to admit about the kind of Daddy he was aching for.

"Wish they'd play with me instead of just watch," Bastian had admitted reluctantly. *"I would love to have a Daddy who chased me round and round, through and over the tubes. It's one of the best parts of watching ferrets play together. It always looks like they are having so much fun 'cause they're not alone in their antics. I— I kinda wish I could find a Daddy who didn't mind being silly sometimes. I'd like to laugh with someone, not just be chuckled at. I'm*

glad I can make them laugh, don't get me wrong, it's just that sometimes I think I'd enjoy them being in on the game."

Daddy William had studied him intently and nodded, flashing him a smile. "There's nothing wrong with that. Just do yourself a favor and don't settle for less. If you do, you're not just setting yourself up for a series of bad experiences, but you're setting your Daddy up to fail too."

He hadn't gotten it, but rather than saying anything he'd just given the barest nod. Fortunately for him, Daddy William was extremely intuitive.

"What I'm getting at is this," he'd gone on to explain, casting his gaze over the lot of them. "If you're doing something that is making you unhappy, eventually, a good Daddy is going to realize that they aren't giving you what they need, and then how do you think that'll make them feel? I'd say pretty damned disappointed, especially if they care deeply for you. The relationship between pet and Daddy is meant to be fluid, cohesive, with each giving the other what they need. It's meant to be a shared experience, with each helping the other become the best version of themselves. If one of you holds back, lies to the other, or pretends to enjoy something simply because they think that is what the other wants, then it isn't going to work out in the long run. Best *bet is to never head down that road. It's a hard thing to come back from."*

Boy was it ever. As he lay there, Bastian found himself wishing there had been a Daddy William in his life before Claude had come along. Then he'd have known better than to get involved with the man in the first place.

You did know better, you did it anyway.

That damned voice in the back of his head was loud as fuck tonight. Grumbling, Bastian rolled on his side and punched the pillow. It wasn't that the voice was wrong, it was just…

He'd been proud of being wanted.

Proud because out of all the other pets, Claude had chosen him and it had been so long since anyone had chosen him for anything.

Pressing the palms of his hands against his eyes, he struggled to hold the tears at bay. The last thing he wanted was for the delivery person to show up with dinner while he was balling his eyes out.

Breathe.

Don't give in to the temptation to revisit old memories. Nothing good ever came of reminding himself of how many times he'd been rejected, left behind or simply walked away from. None of that mattered anymore. He was a different person than he'd been back then. He'd found a way to work around all the issues he'd struggled with in school. He'd proved over and over that he wasn't lazy like his parents had always accused him of being. He could work hard. He could finish things. He could be successful. He just had to do things in a way that worked for him. That was all.

And with sudden clarity, he realized that was the only way things were going to work for him here too. He was going to have to follow his own path, and if it led him to a Daddy, so be it, as long as they accepted him for him.

Chapter 4
How to catch a twisting star

"Excuse me. Sorry about that," Jarrod rambled as he hurried through a trio of guys clustered together near the entrance to the lobby. He narrowly avoided plowing into one, who grumbled at him to slow down before he hurt someone. He wouldn't have to worry about that if people would take their conversations someplace where they wouldn't be blocking people's access to a community space.

Bursting through the doors and into the silvery dawn, he looked left, then right, hoping to get a glimpse of the runner he'd seen dashing down the trail. Of course he was too late to catch him before he reached the fork. Between the elevator and the random obstacles he'd had to dodge, it was no wonder. Damnit all, this was the second day in a row he'd missed out on the chance to catch up to him.

Micki was at work behind the desk, and though he didn't know her well, she'd been there last year when he'd first been hired to train the ponies, and she'd been helpful in directing him to several places he'd been interested in checking out. It might be a longshot, but perhaps touching base with her might give him some clue as to the parkour man's routine, or at the very least, if he had one.

"Morning, Micki, do you have a moment?"

"Sure thing, what can I do for you?"

"Well, I don't know if you've noticed anyone doing flips and spring boarding off things as they went past the window."

"If I had, I'd remember," she said. "At this hour, most people are blinking and trying to wake up, and if they do head out on the walking trail, then it's with a cup of coffee in their hands, or a camera."

"Damn."

"Sorry, I wish I could help you out, but there's only been like, three people down this morning. Those two ladies sitting on the bench out there watching the sun come up, and this guy who was down here reading, but it looks like he left."

Scratching his head, Jarrod struggled to come up with a plan B, wishing he'd had the good sense to get the man's name when they'd bumped into one another. Talk about fortune smiling at him, but then his friend had shown up and whisked him away before Jarrod could say much of anything.

"Is he about yey high with reddish-blond hair, in a hoody and jogging pants," Jarrod asked, holding his hand up to indicate his parkour guy's approximate height.

Her face scrunched up as she gave it some thought before she finally nodded at him. "Actually, yes. I'd say he'd down here about an hour before the sun comes up, sits right over there next to the fireplace."

"Perfect," Jarrod said. It might cost him some sleep but tomorrow morning he'd be seated in the lobby bright and early, thermos of coffee in hand. Maybe he should bring an extra cup, in case the man wished to join him in some before his run, though who accepted random drinks from strangers these days. So maybe forget the cup, at least the first time, so the guy wouldn't think he was a weirdo or something. Mind made up, Jarrod headed back to his room to start his day, confident his plan would yield him the introduction he was after.

^^^

What the hell was that beeping? Groaning, Jarrod sat up and brushed the fine fringe of hair from his eyes. The damned noise was coming from somewhere, but why...damnit, his fist found the offending device and he fumbled to turn it off, grateful when a blessed burst of silence filled the room. Thought faded as his head sunk into the surface of the pillow and he once again nodded off.

^^^

Shit, shit, shit, shit, shit.

Sunlight filled the room and he blinked his eyes against it, cursing himself for forgetting to draw the blinds over the window again. The moment he thought of them, he sprang from the bed, reminded of why he'd left them open these past few days. His parkour running obsession tended to run by super early and he'd...planned to be downstairs with a thermos of coffee before he'd gone on his run this morning, so he could finally introduce himself to him.

Son of a bitch.

One glance at his clock told him it was much too late now. Slamming his fist against the mattress he glared at the ceiling, annoyed that he'd let another opportunity slip through his fingers. Was no need to hurry now. He lay there, grateful it wasn't a training day. His time today was his own, though he had no clue how he was going to spend it. Maybe with a lifting session. He hadn't done legs yet this week. Afterward, well, maybe he'd wander down by the lake once he cleaned up. He could grab a couple sandwiches, perhaps share the crusts with the ducks. It was better than sitting inside and brooding.

Mind made up, Jarrod rolled out of bed, changed, and headed for the elevator in time to see a chattering group wander out, several talking over one another and clearly excited about something. It was only out of the corner of his eye that he noticed the man left behind by their departure and without another thought, he leapt between the doors as they closed, one catching him on the shoulder before it sprang open again, his abruptness clearly startling the man. The moment he recognized Jarrod was clear though. He smiled and raised an eyebrow at his entrance.

"In the interest of fairness, I probably should issue you a warning about elevator doors, considering how kind you were to insure that I took caution not to wander into the lake."

"Perhaps you should."

"Well then, consider this my warning, though I'm not sure if I should be warning you, or the door. Jacked as you are, you might actually be able to do some damage to the poor thing."

Chuckling, Jarrod felt a surge of pleasure wash through him over the man acknowledging his size. As a shorter than average man he'd taken to lifting as a way to even the odds, and it was always an ego boost when someone noticed.

"Thanks, I'll be more careful next time. I wouldn't want to inadvertently wind up trapped in one, though, I doubt it would be too much of a hardship, considering the company."

"Thanks, I think," the man replied as the elevator came to a stop on his floor.

Rather than letting him get away again, Jarrod got off too, unwilling to lose the second chance fate had given him.

"I've seen you on the trail running parkour," Jarrod blurted, stopping the man cold. "Looks like you've been into it awhile too."

"Yeah, ever since I was in high school."

"How'd that happen?"

"Movies, actually. Running track seemed way too disciplined and jogging, well, I can't think of a more boring way to get somewhere, but add a couple backflips in and it completely changes the mood."

"I'll have to take your word for it, but it does look like fun."

"It is if you like your fun with a healthy dose of crashing and burning."

"Seriously? How bad are we talking?"

The man's laugh was smooth and smoky, and the best part of it all was that he didn't seem to be in the slightest bit of a hurry to get away from him. Leaning against the wall beside the vending machine alcove, he appeared completely at ease.

"Well, let's see, I once back flipped off a metal railing and crashed upside down against a concrete wall, like literally, shoulders on the ground, feet against the concrete, wind completely knocked out of me and to add insult to injury, this chipmunk wanders over, sits on my chest and starts chattering at me like he was giving a point by point breakdown of exactly why that move failed."

"No shit?"

"Seriously, I've got a picture on my phone somewhere. A friend took it. It's a little shaky though, considering he was laughing his ass off at me."

"That's friends for ya."

"Tell me about it."

"I'm Jarrod, by the way."

"Bastian, or Bas, it doesn't matter."

"Which do you prefer?"

When Bastian blinked, Jarrod knew it wasn't a question he was used to, almost as if he wasn't used to his wishes mattering.

"Bastian, actually."

"Well then, Bastian, it's very nice to meet you, officially."

"Nice to meet you too."

"So, how, exactly does one get started twisting and flipping over things," Jarrod asked. "I mean, it's one thing to see it in a movie, but I'd imagine you need a gymnastics background or something along those lines so you don't wind up breaking your neck."

"Actually, all you need is a trampoline, a devil may care attitude, and plenty of first aid supplies."

"I'll bet."

Jarrod took note of the way Bastian eyed him up and down, not having to wait long to find out what he was thinking. "No offense, but it might not be the right workout for someone as, well, musclebound as you are. It's more about fluid speed, grace and agility, not strength and power, though you could always use the same surfaces I do, just in a different manner."

"How so?"

"Like, to use for standing or even inclined pushups, or even to do standing jumps onto, though you'd prolly want to consider wraps or braces for your knees at least in the beginning, all that leaping can be a bit hard on the joints."

The depth of his enthusiasm for the sport shone in Bastian's eyes as he spoke, his words punctuated by the way he waved his arms around, rolled his fingers one over the other to emphasize tumbling, and bounced them up and down when he said jump. Jarrod was just about to make a comment about it when Bastian paused in mid-thought, face flushing.

"I am so, so sorry," he blurted, looking adorably flustered. He dropped his hands to his sides and his gaze to the floor as he shifted his weight from one foot to the other. "You asked a simple questions and I went off the rails with details you probably didn't have the slightest interest in. I bet that's the last time you strike up a conversation with someone in an elevator."

"Not at all," Jarrod replied, wishing he knew him well enough to cup him under the chin and raise his face until he could gaze into Jarrod's eyes to see the sincerity in them. "I appreciate your enthusiasm and thoroughly enjoyed the tips you gave as to how I could utilize bits into my own workout. I'm always looking for ways to spice things up. Repetition quickly gets boring."

"Ain't that the truth?"

"Hey, Bastian, there you are. I was waiting for you. So much for being back at eight."

"Yeah, sorry, lost track of time. I had an amazing run and then I started talking to Jarrod. I guess I forgot to check my watch."

"Which you're actually wearing, for pity's sake. What's the point of strapping it to your wrist if you're not even going to look at the blasted thing?"

"Yeah, yeah, I suppose I deserve that for giving you shit about your wallet."

"Yup."

When Bastian turned back toward him, it was with a sheepish look on his face. "It was awesome to meet you, Jarrod. Maybe we'll bump into each other again soon."

"I hope so."

"Well, we're going to be here for the rest of the month."

"Me too."

"Oh, are you hear for the um… the…" Bastian squirmed a little before lowering his voice. "*Pet Play on the Lake* event?"

"Yup. Pony Master Jarrod at your service." Jarrod gave him an impulsive little bow, earning another smile from him.

"Does that mean that ponies are all you play with?" Bastian blurted out, one part saucy and one part curious. He seemed to shock himself a little with the impulsiveness of his own words, and another rosy flush crept over his cheeks, drawing Jarrod's attention to the smattering of freckles across the bridge of his nose.

He didn't try to backtrack though, he just licked his lips and gave a little shrug. "That was probably inappropriate."

"Nope. Only way to find out something you want to know is to ask a question, and to answer yours, yes, at least so far, but that doesn't mean I wouldn't be open to exploring with just the right person, no matter what kind of pet they are."

"I'm not a pony."

"Yeah, I'm pretty sure I already knew that."

Snickering, Bastian rubbed the back of his neck.

"Dude, come on!" Bastian's buddy whined. Jarrod cut him a hard look, hoping he'd get the point and duck back into the room he'd stuck his head out of but no such luck. Instead of retreating he closed the distance between them and caught Bastian's arms. "With as slow as you shower, we're gonna be late."

"Guess I'd better get moving," Bastian said as he was practically dragged back to his room.

"We should get together sometime," Jarrod called after him.

"I'd like that!"

Before Jarrod could nail down a place and a time, Bastian's buddy had propelled him through the doorway of their room and closed the door behind them, leaving Jarrod alone in the hall, shaking his head. Clearly, the friend was more assertive than Bastian, that or Bastian was just easy going enough to let a high-maintenance friend dictate the course of things. Either way, it was clear to Jarrod that getting to know Bastian was going to require finding a place where his friend wasn't going to happen upon them and drag him away.

Nothing close to the building, that was for sure. The trail had promise, though Jarrod hadn't explored all of it yet. There had to be a spot where they could sit uninterrupted and talk for longer than a couple stolen minutes.

Deciding to forgo his trip to the gym in order to explore the walking path, Jarrod took the elevator back to the lobby and strolled out into the sunshine. It truly was a beautiful day, and as he walked along, he began to grasp what Bastian found so appealing about it. There were countless opportunities for him to exercise his skills. The further he got from the lodge, the more secluded the trail grew, with more natural features than man made ones, though he still passed the occasional benches.

The vast majority of them were empty too, and Jarrod could only imagine it would be more so at the time of morning that Bastian made his run. As he rounded a bend in the trail, he came across a familiar figure occupying one.

Tommy looked deep in thought, staring off into the distance with a forlorn look on his face. Seeing that, there was no way Jarrod could just pass him by and continue on his way.

"Something got you down?" he asked, leaning against the edge of the bench. When Tommy glanced his way, and nodded, Jarrod took that as an invitation to sit down. "What's up?"

"Was just thinking about the auction on the final day of the event," Tommy admitted.

"And?"

"I don't think I want to take part."

"Okay. Would you care to tell me why?"

"It's just…all of my gear is kind of ratty. It's second hand and really scuffed up. I got it right before I came out here and I've been working on it each night, trying to follow these tutorials I found on the internet on how to care for leather, but nothing I do is turning out right. I don't want to go into one of the cages looking like a hot mess. No Daddy would ever take a second look at me."

"That could be a problem, but I doubt it would be a deal breaker for most," Jarrod said. "Still, I can understand why it would make you uncomfortable to go out there knowing you weren't looking your best."

"So, it's okay that I don't want to take part?"

"Is that the only reason you don't want to do it?"

"Pretty much. I just don't want to embarrass myself. I'm not the most graceful pony around. Trust me when I say you haven't seen me at my klutziest yet. I'm used to that though. I can handle tripping over my own feet. I've done it enough to know how to pick myself up, dust myself off and laugh at the latest catastrophe, but I was hoping to at least look good while doing it."

Rubbing his chin, Jarrod gave some thought to Tommy's dilemma. While he seemed confident enough with the prospect of a misstep during dressage, the real concern truly seemed to be the leather. It wouldn't do for potential Daddies to think he didn't care enough about his appearance to maintain it right. While some might overlook it, or pose gentle questions, Jarrod knew there were others who would outright snub him for it, as shitty as that might be.

"What if I have a solution to your problem?" Jarrod offered.

"I'll try anything at this point, though I don't have the money to invest in another set of gear. I spent all I could afford to on that set thinking a little polish would make them shine again. Boy was I wrong."

"That's okay, sometimes leather just needs a special bit of know-how to get it looking good again. Videos are great, but what I've got in mind is a boot black and I know just the one who might be able to help. She's arriving in a couple days and I've never known her to turn down a challenge. Why don't you take a couple photos of your gear and send them to me, and I'll forward them along to her, that way she can get a sense of what is wrong with them in case she needs to bring any special products along."

"Oh my god, do you really thing she can help?"

"Well, we won't know until we ask now will we?"

"Nope."

"Here, let me see your phone."

When Tommy passed it over, Jarrod put his contact information in it before he passed it back. "Make sure you take pictures of the worst of it. If there's anyone you don't have to worry about judging you, it's Sasha. She loves leather, especially restoring it to its previous luster. The best part is, she'll teach you how to maintain it in between sessions with a boot black so it'll never end up in that condition again."

"That's awesome. I really appreciate you doing this."

"It's no problem at all. I'm just glad I can help."

"I'm so glad I came out to the event," Tommy said, much of the sadness having bled from his voice, replaced with a hint of hopefulness. "At the club I belong to, there are a bunch of pups and kittens, but no one was into ponies. I always felt like the odd man out, but when I came across the information on this event and the training sessions being offered and saw that there was an entire series devoted to ponies, I just had to find a way to get here. You've really helped me see that I can be happy and comfortable within the community and still be true to myself."

"That's all I ever hoped to accomplish with my lessons."

"Thank you. I'll get those pictures to you as soon as I get back to my room," Tommy said, popping up off the bench. Enthusiasm had replaced the gloominess that had settled over his features, and as he waved and took off running, Jarrod couldn't help but hope he was one of the lucky ones who found his Daddy this year. It seemed to Jarrod that he could do with some long-term encouragement and understanding, now if only the right Daddy would come along and give it to him.

Chapter 5
Hedge jumps and breakfast picnics

Diving over the last hedge, Bastian tucked his head and landed in a forward role, popping up on his feet as soon as he'd completed it. Laughter bubbled up from his throat, so he let it roll out of him, boisterous and loud, as he spun around in circles, the exhilaration of a successful run leaving him giddy. The walk back would settle him down, but he wasn't ready to shed the feeling yet, not when it still washed over his skin like pinpricks of static electricity.

"Bravo," a voice called out, followed by enthusiastic clapping that brought a bit of heat to Bastian's face. He turned slower this time, enough to let his eyes focus and his brain register that he wasn't alone. Jarrod sat on a colorful picnic blanket several feet away, containers spread out in front of him like he was about to settle in for a feast.

"I–I" Bastian stammered, stunned into inaction. "I'm so sorry. I didn't expect anyone to be using this spot this early. I'll just get out of here and leave you to your meal. Sorry to come crashing in on you, again."

"Well, in this case, your presence was not only expected, it was anxiously anticipated," Jarrod admitted, leaving Bastian frowning and a bit confused.

"You were waiting for me? Why?"

"Because our conversation yesterday got interrupted and I didn't want to miss out on another opportunity to talk to you," Jarrod admitted. "For the past few mornings I've watched you running beneath my window, but when I tried to catch up with you yesterday, I got up too late. Running into you in the elevator was just pure, dumb luck, but it didn't last nearly long enough, so I figured I'd set up on the most likely spot on the trail and hope you showed up."

"And what would you have done if I hadn't?"

"Picked another spot again tomorrow and tried again."

"Oh."

"That…probably sounded way more stalkerish than I intended," Jarrod admitted, the look on his face more grimace than smile.

There was a faint blush there too, which Bastian found endearing, if only because the man was supposed to be a Master and a trainer and yet here he sat, looking slightly uncomfortable talking to him. It was enough to make Bastian feel powerful and desired. After all, it wasn't every day that someone went this far out of their way to do something special just for him.

"I tried to pick a spot far enough away from the lodge that you wouldn't be cutting your run too short by joining me," Jarrod said, appearing hopeful. "I hope I didn't underestimate."

"No, I um, this was the end of my run, actually. The trail is much too long to make a full circuit, at least, not with the speed and vigor I tend to run it."

"That's what I guessed, but you know how assumptions work, half the time you get bit in the ass by them."

"Well, this was definitely one time when you didn't."

"Does that mean you'll join me?"

"Yeah, I'd umm, like that. I can't remember the last time I was on a picnic."

"Then by all means, have a seat," Jarrod said, gesturing to the empty spot across from him. "I wasn't sure what all you might like, so I brought a bit of everything, though, nothing too heavy. I figured, if you were anything like me, you wouldn't want to overload on carbs after a run so it's mostly just fruit, some boiled eggs, bacon, and a couple chocolate chip muffins."

As he spoke, he removed the lids from each of the containers, revealing a bounty of fresh fruit that left Bastian's mouth watering. "Holy shit that looks good."

"I'm glad you approve."

"Oh my god, I more than approve, is that honeydew?"

"Yup."

"It's my favorite."

"Good to know," Jarrod said as he nudged the container towards him until Bastian got the hint and took a piece. It damn near melted in his mouth, juicy, sweet, with all the rich, melony flavor the fruit was known for. There was nothing more disappointing than biting into a piece that was under-ripe and tasted like water, or worse, nothing at all. This one was perfect. Before he could stop himself, Bastian let out an obscene moan, and reached for another piece, licking the dripping juice off his fingers and sucking them for good measure.

"Damn."

His eyes popped open to see Jarrod watching him, a strawberry poised between his fingers, halfway to his mouth. He seemed to have forgotten about it though, as he stared at Bastian's unintended show. Shrugging, Bastian couldn't find it in himself to be embarrassed, the melon was too good, and it had been months since he'd had one, so he plucked another piece and ate it a bit less messily, though not by much.

"I guess I picked a good one," Jarrod said as Bastian sat the carton back down.

As tempting as it was to keep on eating, he didn't want to be rude and hog all the pieces, especially when there was so much more fruit to sample.

"Ohhh yeah. It's always hit or miss when I choose one," Bastian admitted. "I've thumped my way through a stack of them and left thinking I got a good one, only to cut into it and discover it really wasn't ready yet."

"See, now that's where you went about it wrong," Jarrod said, taking a piece for himself while Bastian tried the cantaloupe. Like the honeydew it was perfect, cold too, and just firm enough that the flavors burst against his tongue.

"How do you mean?"

"Thumping works for watermelon, but on some of the other melons, it's better to pick them up and smell the end. The better the scent, the more ready it is. If you can't smell anything, or it's really faint, that isn't the melon for you, not unless you like biting into a juicy chunk of lightly flavored water."

Bastian shook his head, glad he wasn't the only one who'd had such a disappointing experience. "No thanks, it sucks when that happens. Especially when they stop ripening once they're picked so even letting them sit isn't going to help anything."

"Exactly."

"Oh yum, blackberries."

"Yeah, they had quite a selection at the grocery store last night," Jarrod admitted. "I couldn't have wished for any better."

"I'm still blown away that you did this."

"Why?"

"'Cause people don't go out of their way to do things like this for me."

"Their loss."

"When you say it like that, it's easy to believe you mean it."

"Good, 'cause I do."

He said it with such certainty; he left little doubt in Bastian's mind that he was telling the truth. Still, there was that tiny, lingering voice ringing with pessimism, reminding him to be cautious and not be so eager to trust.

"So, where are you from?" Jarrod asked. "Was this a long or short trip for you?"

"Spokane. Would have been a short flight but Chauncy and I decided to turn it into a road trip so all in all, it took a little over a day, but only fifteen hours of it were driving. We made some stops along the way, tried some amazing chocolates, and damn near poisoned ourselves on the subs from hell. We made up for it with some stellar donuts though, like seriously, out of this world. Who'd have ever thought to put breakfast cereal on them?"

"Okay, that does sound delicious," Jarrod admitted. "I've had candy bar covered ones, but I've never seen anything like you're describing."

"Neither had I, until we popped in there. The whole visit was an experience."

"Don't you just love happening on something unique like that?"

"Oh hell yeah. Back home, I make it a habit to check out all the new spots when they pop up," Bastian admitted. "And not just food places either, I'm talking escape rooms, rage rooms, climbing walls, skate parks, whitewater rafting, zip lining, the snowboard park, and as many of the trails as I can manage. I've been to the arboretum several times, the Japanese garden and the koi ponds, which, talk about a beautiful place to just sit and think. I spent hours there generating ideas for a client's project."

"Really, and what kind of work do you do?"

"Graphic design. I'm self-taught and self-employed, which was a lot of trial and error, but I've finally built up a good client base. Mostly I design logos, menu layouts, advertisements, that sort of thing, but the best part is being my own boss."

There was a look in Jarrod's eyes that Bastian found impossible to read, though if he had to venture a guess, he'd say it was a mix of curiosity and humor.

"Does that mean you're not fond of taking orders?"

"Nope, just means I'm particular about who I take orders from, though, that isn't the only reason I prefer working on my own."

"Okay. And the other reasons?"

Quirking his lips in as much of a smile as he could manage, Bastian gave a half-hearted shrug and popped a blackberry in his mouth to avoid answering right away. When he reached for another though, Jarrod moved the carton just out of reach and wagged a finger at him.

"Now you're stalling. It can't be that bad, unless you're gonna tell me you went on an office rampage and put laxatives in everyone's cocoa, or replaced everyone's mouses with Jell-O versions of them."

Bastian opened his mouth, then snapped it closed again, 'casue who the hell even thought of something like that?

"What?" Jarrod asked with a shrug and a wink.

"All I was gonna say was that I have a hard time sitting still, no way I could park my ass in a chair all day and just work," Bastian admitted. "I gotta say though, those are some pretty creative ways to fuck with people, well, at least the

Jell-O one, the laxatives are kinda cruel, don't you think? Tell me you didn't really do that?"

"The Jell-O I did, the laxatives, no, though I thought about it, especially with this one boss," Jarrod admitted. "Nothing any of us ever did was right according to him, mostly 'cause he kept changing his mind about what he wanted. I was so glad to leave that job and move on to a better one. If I'd stuck around too much longer, laxatives might have been the least of his worries."

"Really?"

"It would have gotten me fired, I'm sure, but I was on the verge of completely tanking a project, as in totally fucking it up in every way imaginable, just so he'd look like the ass he was when he took it before the department heads. He was always claiming credit for everything, no matter how many of us worked on something, or who tossed out which idea, so I figured why not let him go in boasting about that little mess and see how things went for him."

"Sounds like he would have gotten exactly what he deserved."

"True but getting fired might have cost me a chance at the job I have now, and I love it there."

"Is it another office job?"

"God, no, I had more than enough of the corporate backstabbing to last a lifetime," Jarrod explained. "Climbing the ladder of success might sound nice when you're fresh out of college, but once you've been in the workforce for a while, you start to learn that the climb almost always comes at someone else's expense. I wanted to do something meaningful that I could truly be proud of, so I took a job as a community service manager and work on developing programs that benefit people."

"Whoa, that's pretty awesome. Did you have to go back to school for that?"

"Nah, everything covered in the job description was something I'd already been doing for years, only now, I get to see how the work I do is helping people, which is a damn good feeling."

"I bet."

Bastian munched as he listened to Jarrod's story and the birds sing-songing from the trees. A cheerful ruckus, they were clearly enjoying the morning, as was Bastian, who stretched out on his side, sighed, and reached for one of the eggs.

"I brought some garlic salt if you'd like," Jarrod offered. "I think I've got a packet or two of plain laying around too, if you'd prefer."

"Actually, I'd love the garlic one."

Bastian sprinkled it lightly on the outside of his egg once Jarrod passed it over, nibbling it while staring at the way the sunrays brought out the highlights in Jarrod's hair. He was a ruggedly handsome man, with gentle eyes and a kind air about him that made it easy to relax in his presence.

"This is way nicer than the restaurant back in the lodge," Bastian said, sighing contently. "Not that there's anything wrong with it or the food, it's fine, it's just, here isn't crowded and full of other people's conversations."

"I'd love to do it again if you'd be up for it."

Joy surged through him at the offer. Despite the lingering tiredness left over from his workout, just the thought of another morning like this had him jazzed. "Are you kidding? I'd love to, only next time, you've got to let me know when, so I can bring something too."

"Nope. Uh-uh. Then I wouldn't get to enjoy the look of surprise on your face when you summersaulted right in the middle of it."

"Well, technically, it was more like the edge."

"Still, I loved how thrilled you were when you realized all this was for you."

Warmth flooded him and left him feeling like he was someone precious and desired. Of all the people here, it was his company Jarrod had sought out, and apparently not just once either.

"How many years have you been coming here?" Bastian blurted, a sobering thought flashing like ice water through his head.

"This is my second. I trained the ponies last year too and before you ask, no, I've never done this before. Most of my free time last year was spent on the lake, canoeing, or up in my room working on some projects for work."

"I brought a few projects along myself," Bastian replied, nibbling his bottom lip. "How'd you know what I was going to ask?"

"Your expression changed," Jarrod admitted. "One minute you were completely at ease, the next your eyes darkened, and I could see you tensing up when you were asking the question."

"Sorry."

"Don't be, it was a legitimate question. I'm well aware that there are people who attend events like this just to try to hook up with as many people as possible, but that's never been me. I came because I genuinely care about the pony community. Coming here and training the ponies is my way of helping it thrive."

"If you're anything like Daddy William, then I bet you're pretty amazing."

"I've never have the privilege of sitting in on one of his training sessions, but I've only heard good things about him."

"He's awesome. He's been nothing but encouraging to me," Bastian admitted. "I don't know if I would have had the courage to sign up for the auction if it wasn't for him."

"Really?"

"Yeah."

"Want to tell me why?"

Squirming, Bastian scanned the containers and snagged the last piece of that beautiful honeydew melon before answering. "Guess I never really saw myself as being a good pet, at least, not the way so many others are soft and compliant and content to curl in their Master's arms and be everything their Masters want them to be."

While Jarrod sat rubbing his chin and staring at him, Bastian popped the melon in his mouth, chewed and wondered if he'd just revealed a bit of information about himself that would render him undesirable in the other man's eyes.

"There's nothing wrong with being the snuggly, cuddly sort of pet that lives for praise and only does what someone else tells them too," Jarrod explained. "Some people need that kind of structure in their lives, so it works for them. The important thing to remember is that is doesn't work for everyone and if it doesn't work for you then that's okay, it doesn't have to. You choose what kind of pet you want to be."

Bastian's lips split into a huge smile, and what tension he'd started feeling drained out of him again. "I was right, you are like Daddy William. That's pretty much what he said too."

"Good. Uniqueness should be preserved, not forced into an unbending mold until there's nothing left that makes a person special. In fact, I get the feeling you're full of surprises, in and out of pet space, which is why I'd love the opportunity to get to know you better, and not just out here on the trail, either. That is, if you'd be up for it."

"Hell yeah."

"In that case, why don't we plan something for tomorrow afternoon, unless Chauncy already has you roped into something."

"Nope, he's got a training session with the kittens, so he'll be busy."

"And if you're in Daddy William's group, then yours is this afternoon at two, right?" Jarrod asked.

"Uh-huh."

"Do you mind me asking what kind of pet you are?" Jarrod asked. "I'd heard that he had a couple koalas, a turtle, a dragon, a bird, a ferret and even a mouse and a rabbit in his group this year."

"I'm the ferret."

Jarrod beamed at him and nodded, glancing toward the hedge and back again. "That doesn't surprise me at all. In fact, I can just imagine you rolling over one of the big foam logs in the playroom, your ears bobbing as your tail swayed."

"I love the giant tunnels too, it's one of the best parts. Not only can I run through it, but I can get inside it and roll around too, though I have to be careful I don't run into anyone else. Sometimes, when I start playing, I get a little rambunctious and forget that not everyone likes to play like that," Bastian admitted. "Sometimes it's hard to stay in the right headspace when I start worrying about crashing into someone."

"I can only imagine that would be difficult."

"Yeah."

"What does Daddy William do when you start to play a little bit wild?"

"Puts himself between me and the others and directs me back into the part of the play space he's kind of designated for me. It's got cool stuff to play with, and on, and sometimes one of the koalas joins in with me. He likes to climb things and swing off them so Daddy William has several things set up for the both of us, like cargo netting we can climb and a swing. I love to spin around in it and get all dizzy and wobbly."

"Sounds like fun."

"It really is."

"So, what would you like to do tomorrow? We can do anything you'd like, though I'd prefer it be something that will allow us to keep getting to know one another."

"How about canoeing?" Bastian suggested. "I've been dying to go out on the lake. Maybe you could show me some of your favorite spots."

"I'd love to. It's a date then. Meet me at the boat launch at ten?"

"I'll be there."

"Perfect. And Bastian."

"Yeah?"

"Thanks again for having breakfast me."

Chapter 6
When worry grips your soul

Ten-ten and Jarrod checked the contents of the picnic basket for the fourth time since arriving at the boat launch that morning. Nothing had shifted, everything was still in place. He wedged the basket beneath one of the seats and checked that the oars were properly placed in their rings. Everything was good to go, everything but his date.

Scanning the expanse of grass laid out between him and the lodge, Jarrod squinted, hoping to spot that familiar shimmer of hair, but so far, nothing. He knew he should have asked to put his number in Bastian's phone and requested he do the same. That way they could at least touch base with one another if plans had changed.

Had he come on too strong? Been too forward with that impromptu picnic? No, he didn't think that was it. Bastian didn't strike him as a shrinking violet too afraid to speak up if something felt off to him. At the very least, he'd have walked away without a backward glance if he wasn't interested. Instead, he'd stayed even after the food was gone, laughing and listening. The encounter had certainly left Jarrod with high hopes for this morning's outing, though they were slowly beginning to fade as the minutes ticked by without any sign of Bastian.

Could he have hurt himself during his run this morning? Spun a little too fast and crashed into a tree? He'd watched enough videos of parkour fails to know what could happen if someone timed a jump wrong or failed to stick the landing. Maybe he was lying stunned or broken out there just waiting for someone to come along and find him.

The thought sent a cold shiver down Jarrod's spine as anxiety surged through him. He glanced at the path, then back at the canoe, deciding the basket would just have to stay where it was while he went to check. If anything, it might catch Bastian's attention if he showed up late and encourage him to wait around for Jarrod to get back.

Mind made up, Jarrod hurried toward the path, thoughts tormenting him with a scrambled array of images—Bastian's blood covered face, a gash on the side of his head oozing, Bastian clutching his leg, bone broken and unable to support his weight, Bastian pale and unconscious between the hedges, unable to call out for help, Bastian—

"Jarrod! Hey, Jarrod! Wait up."

He heard the words, but he wasn't in the mood to wait, not one minute longer. Bastian could be in need of medical assistance, and Jarrod would make damn certain he got it.

"Jarrod!"

It was the glint of gold-red that drew his attention to the flushed, flustered face of the very man he'd been fretting about. Bastian doubled over, hands on his knees, struggling for breath, which told Jarrod that he must have been sprinting just to catch up to him.

"I am...so...sorry...I'm...late."

He panted between each word, hair not only wet and disheveled, but dripping into his face.

"G-got back...to my room...after..."

"Take a moment and catch your breath, then you can tell me," Jarrod said, having to lace his hands behind his back so he wouldn't rub circles on Bastian's.

Each inhale sounded ragged, each exhale a harsh and rapid woosh. Bastian straightened up a little, groaned and swiped the water from his eyes, appearing a tad grumpy.

"Didn't you hear me calling you?" he panted, straightening to his full height.

"No. I was too busy picturing you a crumpled wreck somewhere along the trail."

"Shit," Bastian huffed. "Guess that's two things I've got to be sorry for. Didn't mean to worry you. I never intended to be late, either. I'd have text and warned you, but I never got your number."

"Yeah, I thought of that myself, somewhere between the third and fifth time I looked at my phone."

"Sorry."

"It happens, besides, it wasn't your fault I got all in a tizzy picturing you somewhere hurt, that was my own imagination running away from me."

"Still wouldn't have happened if I'd been on time."

"True," Jarrod said. "You're not about to cancel on me, are you?"

"Hell no. I've been looking forward to this since yesterday," Bastian said.

"In that case, let's go," Jarrod said, leading the way back to the boat ramp where their canoe was still waiting for them.

The model was perfect. A wooden two-seater with a single set of oars and a high-backed seat near the bow that allowed for them to sit face to face. It was a good thing too, this way he could study Bastian and the myriad expressions that flashed across those tanned and freckled features.

"So what happened?" Jarrod asked after the third time Bastian tried to smile only to have it fade a moment later, replaced by a narrow-eyed scowl.

He sighed heavily, propped his head on his hand and his elbow on his thigh, staring half at the water and half at him in a way that suggested to Jarrod that he was considering whether or not to answer.

"It's too beautiful a morning to rehash that shit again," Bastian said at last, though Jarrod didn't miss the uncertainty in his voice. There was just enough there to suggest he should push a little and see if he couldn't get Bastian to open up.

"Did something go wrong on your run?"

"Nah, it was perfect. Warm enough that I didn't need my hoodie, cool enough that I didn't overheat in a long-sleeved t-shirt. I ran the forested section with that cluster of gazeboes. It was closer to the lodge than my usual route while still offering plenty of trees to springboard off of. Figured I'd up the intensity level while cutting the time, which would still give me a chance to clean up and get in a little nap before meeting you.

Jarrod chuckled. "And let me guess, you overslept?"

"No, I wouldn't still be dripping like a rain-soaked mongoose if that was the case," Bastian admitted. "Though I kinda wish it was. At least then, I'd have gotten some peace."

"Uh-oh, the way you said that suggests a distinct lack of it."

"Because there was, and honestly, I don't know if I handled the situation the right way, especially since I was in a hurry for it to end. Only now I feel like a shithead for being so snippy with Chauncy, but damn it all, I just—"

Grumbling, Bastian threw up his hands and muttered an impressive stream of curses.

"You two aren't together, are you?" Jarrod asked, a pang of uncertainty rippling through him. He was seriously going to be disappointed if that was the case.

The way Bastian snorted and shook his head, eyes going wide as if he couldn't fathom why Jarrod would think that was all the answer he needed.

"He's kinda high maintenance sometimes, but you seriously couldn't ask for a better friend. I just wish he could see what a good guy he is instead of putting himself down all the time, then it would be way easier to talk to him."

"Let me guess, this morning was one of those times?"

"Oh yeah, and he wasn't just badmouthing himself this time either, he was having a complete meltdown and trying to pack his bags and take off. He actually promised to come back and get me when the event was over, not that I was going to let him just walk away and miss out, but damn, the timing sucked, since all of this was happening while I was trying to unwind and get ready."

"Is this his first time at an event like this?"

"It's both of ours."

Nodding, Jarrod rowed them further away from shore, torn between wanting to help Bastian help his friend, and wanting him to put his morning behind him so they could enjoy their time together.

"Whoa…"

The breathy sound of surprise drew Jarrod's attention to the majestic bird perched on one leg at the edge of the water. It was so still that for a moment he thought it was nothing more than a lawn ornament, then it ducked its head beneath the water with predatory grace and emerged with a fish in its beak.

"Cool, huh?"

"Oh yeah," Bastian said, gaze lingering on the bird. Jarrod's was too, the fish soon disappearing down its gullet. Once it had, the heron resumed its pose, waiting for another one.

"If we're lucky, we might see an eagle circling," Jarrod said. "I saw a few last year and they were utterly breathtaking."

"Now that would be a sight. I've only seen one once and it was perched way up in a tree beside this huge nest. Talk about majestic."

"I know, right."

When Bastian tilted his head up to look at the sky, Jarrod caught a glimpse of several colorful lines of ink peeking out from beneath the top of his t-shirt. While he couldn't make out what the design was, it piqued his curiosity enough to hope that one day he'd get an up close and personal look at it; maybe even trace the lines with his tongue.

Down boy! he chided himself.

"I forgot how quiet it can be away from shore," Bastian said still staring up at the clouds. "A week ago a month by the lake had seemed like an amazing idea, now I'm not so sure I was prepared for going that long with a roomie."

His voice had taken on a soft, almost wistful tone, and it occurred to Jarrod that he'd been right in thinking he could learn a lot about the man by being out here with him. "Gets trying after a while, doesn't it?"

"Especially in a space the size of a hotel room," Bastian replied. "The only place I get any privacy, aside from on my morning runs, is in the shower, and let me tell you, I spend at least a half hour in there."

"How long have you lived alone?"

"Six years. I went from my folk's place, which was crowded as hell, to a rooming house, where at least I had a space of my own and a door with a lock on it. Two years there and I'd saved up enough to rent a loft. I've been there ever since. Best part is it's right above a bakery which closes at four every afternoon. It's never loud, it always smells good, and the only neighbor is an author who likes things just as quiet as I do."

"Damn, sounds like paradise, or at least, as close as anyone can find living in the city."

"No shit. I couldn't imagine moving unless it was to someplace quiet and remote like this," Bastian said. "Then I wouldn't be able to pack my boxes fast enough."

"It does have its appeal, doesn't it?"

"Yeah, it does. Just the thought of swaying in a hammock, reading a book or soaking up the heat of a campfire is the most perfect image in the world. Add in a bubbling little brook, some pan-fried trout and the right person to share it with, and it'd be heaven on earth."

Until Bastian had mentioned having a person to share his scenic vision with, Jarrod had feared he was going to declare his desire to become a recluse with only some songbirds and a couple cats for company. The fact that he expressed interest in having a special person in his life gave Jarrod hope that if they proved compatible, it could be him. After all, the vision Bastion was describing held a great deal of appeal for Jarrod too. The city, for all the good he did within his community, had its moments when it was taxing, and even stressful to live in. Just a week before coming out here the office he worked in had been vandalized by someone who hadn't like the fact that they'd created an after-school program for LGBTQ youth.

"I swear I'm not as anti-social as I make myself sound," Bastian said, chuckling a little.

"Hey, sometimes it's nice to get away from the craziness of people," Jarrod replied. "A little wood smoke, some tasty fish, a deer path to wander down, it all sounds beautiful to me. I've lived in the city all my life, but that doesn't mean I don't dream of someplace less hectic."

"My grandfather used to take me and my siblings camping in the summer when school was out," Bastian said. "It was just about the only time I didn't feel like a complete fuckup. Put me in a classroom and I was lost. My folks were forever getting called in because I was constantly distracted and couldn't get anything done, but no one ever wanted to hear that being there was overwhelming. There was too much going on. Home was the same way, too. In the woods though, I could always find someplace to sit where I could hear my own thoughts and not everyone else's."

"How many siblings do you have, anyway?"

"Six, plus my cousin Glen came to live with us when he was four."

Jarrod let out a low whistle, unable to imagine what it would be like to share a house with so many people.

"How about you?" Bastian asked. "You got any siblings?"

"Yeah, just one though," Jarrod explained. "A sister, but she's twelve years older than me. She was out of the house before I was out of elementary school, so it's not like we spent a lot of time together."

"Man, that sounds awesome. It was three of us to a room until my oldest brother moved out, then Glen moved into that room with my brother Steve, which left me and Terry to share, which wasn't so bad, since he was always doing after school stuff so at least I had some time by myself before he came home. It sucked for my sisters though, the three of them had to share a room until enough of us boys moved out."

"Damn, that's…a lot."

"Tell me about it."

"So, were you born in Spokane or did you just relocate there?"

"Nope, born and raised in the city. My mom's family was from Liberty Lake, which is where we'd go camping in summer, but when my grandfather's store failed, he and my grandmother moved a couple blocks from us, otherwise, I'd have moved up there when I moved out."

"I didn't move too far from where I grew up, either," Jarrod admitted.

"Where was that?"

"Bellingham," Jarrod replied. "Looks like we are both Washingtonians."

"That's near the border, right?"

"Yup?"

"Have you ever crossed up into Vancouver?"

"All the time. It's beautiful up there."

"That's what I've heard," Bastian admitted. "I'm planning my first trip for early next year to Dine Out, Vancouver."

"I hear the food is amazing. I've considered heading up to it myself."

"Have you ever lived anywhere else besides Bellingham?" Bastian asked. His eyes were bright and focused on Jarrod. In fact, he looked to be thoroughly enjoying the conversation, which was promising.

"Spent six years away in college and decided that was long enough. Came home with a master's degree and delusions of being an executive by the time I was thirty. I already told you how that turned out."

"Yup, and it sounds like you're happier for it."

"You're damn right I am."

"Ain't it funny how doing one thing different can change your whole life?" Bastian mused.

"Sometimes that's all it takes."

"See, I keep trying to tell that to Chauncy," Bastian said, his attention shifting from the sky back to him.

Jarrod could see the change in him though. The once grumpy frown had been replaced with a calm stillness and the barest hint of a smile. Serene, that's the way he looked as they floated along, Jarrod occasionally rowing as they talked.

"And he's not getting it," Jarrod pondered aloud.

"I'm not even sure if he wants to get it," Bastian admitted. "It's almost starting to feel like he's determined to give up just because things aren't happening as fast as he wants them too. I guess that's what happens when you grow up privileged and used to having everything go your way."

"Ahh, one of those."

Bastian clearly didn't appreciate the tone in his voice; his eyes narrowed even as he puffed up a bit.

"I'm not putting down your friend," Jarrod hurried to assure him. "It's just that I know the type you're describing, and sometimes it takes more than words to get them to see any side but their own."

"Yeah."

Seeing him deflate left Jarrod hoping he was open to accepting some advice on how to help his friend. "Seems to me like you're already doing the best thing you can for him by listening. Just make sure you don't sacrifice your own desires in the process. I'm not saying that he's a time suck because I don't know him, but the two times I've encountered him, he's come off as a bit demanding of your time, which isn't always a good thing."

"You're not wrong. He's awesome to be around when things are going good for him, but when they aren't…"

"He sucks all the fun out of the room," Jarrod supplied.

"Pretty much."

"So what's the issue that had him looking to bail out of the event?"

"I guess there's a bratty kitty in the kitten group that's been taking up all the trainer's attention and Chauncy wasn't handling it well," Bastian explained. "He's already got issues with being ignored at the club we belong to, so to have it happen here, well, he was super upset about it. I got him mostly settled down, but it took more time than I wanted it to which was why I was late meeting up with you."

"That's not supposed to happen here," Jarrod said, feeling a touch of irritation himself. "If that's really going on the way your friend described, then that could be a problem."

Bastian squirmed a little, something Jarrod was coming to quickly mean he was feeling a uncomfortable about something. "It's Chauncy. I love the guy to death but I don't know if he's being overly sensitive, or if there really is an issue. Hell, the other day he told me he was jealous of me and my ex, despite being the one to constantly point out what a shit person Claude was, so it's hard to know what to make of everything he was saying."

Jarrod could understand Bastian's reluctance. When someone was known for being a drama queen, or overly sensitive, it was hard to know when to take their claims seriously. Still, there were ways to suss out the truth and ensure that every pet in attendance had the most positive experience possible. Even a seasoned trainer could find themselves inadvertently paying too much attention to a pet that needed a great deal of help. If a pet was deliberately being bratty, and a trainer was letting it happen to the detriment of the others in the group, then that was something that would need to be addressed sooner rather than later. At the very least, it bore some looking into.

Bastian let his fingers trail over the surface of the water, a devilish look crossing his face seconds before he flicked water Jarrod's way, jarring him out of his thoughts.

"What was that for?" Jarrod replied even as he splashed back.

Bastian punctuated his answer with a splash of his own. "Brooding."

"Hey now, you were doing it first," Jarrod replied, retaliating.

Words disintegrated into laughter as they splashed cold lake water at one another until it dripped from their hair and down their faces. Maybe it was immature and beneath them, but as far as Jarrod was concerned, it was just a wonderful part of an awesome, amazing day.

Chapter 7
Curled beneath the stars

Their afternoon on the water transitioned to an evening spent lying on a blanket, staring up at the stars. Somewhere along the line, Jarrod had reached for his hand and Bastian had entwined their fingers, the heat from their palms pressed together helping to keep him warm as cooler temperatures crept in.

Bastian couldn't remember the last time conversation with anyone had been this easy. They hopped from one topic to the next, laughing at the similarities in their tastes and occasionally debating the differences. Never had Bastian felt so at ease getting to know someone. With Claude, the man had talked on and on about himself until Bastian started to feel like he was downloading his life story while barely giving Bastian a chance to respond. Before that, there had been Lyle, with whom conversation had felt like a chore, one he was forcing the man to endure every time he said something to him. While the physical had been nice, thrilling even, that's all it had been. Wild but empty and completely devoid of emotional connection, unsatisfying in the end, despite how persistent Lyle had been, showing up on his doorstep even after Bastian had declared it over.

Too little, too late, especially when the wine and half-dead houseplant had all felt like empty gestures, a ploy just to have sex with him again.

"We should think about going in, you're starting to tremble," Jarrod suggested, drawing Bastian out of his thoughts.

"I'm not ready for the evening to end."

"It doesn't have to. We can always go up to my room and find something to watch, or just sprawl across the bed and keep on talking. To tell the truth, I'm not in a hurry to be rid of you."

Sighing, Bastian considered the offer, even while wiggling into a slightly more comfortable position on the blanket. "Just a little while longer."

"Okay, but if you start full on shivering, that's it, we're going in," Jarrod declared.

"Yes, Sir," Bastian muttered, so easy and automatic he wasn't sure which of them he surprised more with it. "I...sorry, that just slipped out."

"Nothing to be sorry about. I didn't mind in the slightest."

"I'm not a pony."

"I know."

"I'm nothing like one."

"I know that too."

"I never wanted a trainer to teach me to do tricks or follow commands."

"Okay. What *do* you want?"

Humming, Bastian thought about that. It might be best to lay everything on the line before he grew too attached to moments like this. "I don't want someone who is going to act like they're okay with me being me, then later try and change me. Claude used to do that shit, and I hated it 'cause I always ended up feeling like I was a disappointment to him."

"How so?"

"Just…he loved to show me off. Called me his pretty pet. He'd bring ribbons and tie them in bows around my neck or the ears of my outfit, and he loved to spend time brushing my hair and the fur of my suit. Problem was, I hated sitting still for it and I was always getting ruffled. When it happened at play nights he'd lecture me the whole way home, or worse, give me the silent treatment, either way sucked. When I asked why he didn't just find someone better suited for him, he'd always tell me he didn't want anyone else, he wanted me and that I should learn to do better. Felt like I'd been hearing that all my life."

"You mentioned something like that earlier, about school and your parents thinking you weren't trying hard enough," Jarrod said.

"'Cause they were always saying I needed to apply myself more and study harder, that I would do better if I just buckled down and focused on my tasks. It wasn't until I was halfway through high school that a guidance counselor suggested I get tested for ADD."

"Did it turn out you have it?"

"Big time. I tried meds for a little while, but I hated the way they made me feel. Figured I was better off just being me and figuring out what worked and what didn't. I might have sucked at the core classes, but I was awesome at art and took every elective I could fit in. Graphic design was my favorite though. I'd find these video tutorials and practice with them until I got good at a particular technique, then I'd work out how to mesh it with the stuff I'd learned before. It's an ongoing process. I still watch videos and practice when I'm not working on something for someone."

"Kind of like your parkour."

"Yeah."

"Sounds to me like you learn best through repetition, and watching how something is done."

"Pretty much. I watch tons of videos on a parkour technique before I ever try to incorporate it into my routine."

"And what did you do when you started to explore being a pet?"

"Attended a lot of munches," Bastian admitted. "Even then I still wasn't sure if it was for me. Coming here really has changed that though. I know now that there are all different kinds of Daddies and trainers out there the same as there are pets and that communication and honesty are really important before you just jump into something with someone. That's where I messed up before. I was so hung up on the thrill of being wanted that I never stopped to think about if I was wanted by the right person for me."

"I'd say that's pretty important in the grand scheme of things."

"Yeah." Bastian fell quiet for several seconds as a shooting star streaked across the sky. He made a quick wish, giving Jarrod's hand a squeeze as he plunged ahead with the rest of his thoughts. "So um, if you're not good with everything I've told you about the kind of pet I am, then um, maybe this should be the last time we hang out like this. I don't wanna start liking you too much if I'm just destined to disappoint you."

"Fortunately for the both of us, that isn't the case," Jarrod replied. "And for the record, I would love the opportunity to show you. There is an open play session Saturday night if you'd care to join me. We can test the waters and see how we mesh."

Could it be that easy, could he already be getting his wish? "I'd love that."

"Good. Ready to head in now?"

"Not really, but if it's getting too chilly for you, we can."

"I'm good. I'm the one with the jacket on, remember?"

"True."

"Just remember what I said about you shivering, I meant that shit."

"I know." And the best part was, Bastian did. The vehemence in Jarrod's voice made him feel safe and protected. He waited for irritation to hit, but it never did. Maybe it was because Jarrod wasn't badgering him or trying to get him to change his mind. He was good with being there with him, and his one demand, that they go in if Bastian started shivering, was a reasonable enough request. One that showed he cared, too.

"You know, I think it might help things if I were to tell you about the type of pony I've always been drawn to,"

Jarrod began, his words drawing Bastian's undivided attention. "How much about pony play do you know?"

"Just um, that there are hoods and harnesses and carriages to pull and all kinds of steps the ponies do when they're being shown off," Bastian replied.

"That's part of it," Jarrod said. "There's a lot more, like there is with any pet. I've always been drawn to the ponies who were spirited and headstrong. The high energy ones that others might not take the time to work with because first you've got to figure out how to get them to settle down into the right headspace before you can work with them. I love a pony who knows their own mind, needs a light hand on the reins and to be given their head more often than not. I've always appreciated a pony who wants to be part of a team rather than being led about. Now, who does that sound like?"

Bastian didn't need to think about it, the answer was obvious. "Me."

"Exactly. It makes no difference what kind of gear you wear, you're still all of the things I enjoy in a pet, and I want to continue getting to know you," Jarrod replied. "Earlier tonight I asked what kind of trainer, what kind of Daddy you were hoping to find, but instead of answering me, all you did was tell me what you didn't want. I'm not even sure if you noticed that or not."

"It just seemed easier."

"I don't know about easy, but it is helpful to know. I'm still hoping you'll answer the original question though."

Bastian opened his mouth, then snapped it closed when a cold wind rustled the trees around him. There was no denying the temperature change now or the effort it was taking to tough it out.

"Would it be okay if I waited until after we were in your room to answer that?" Bastian asked, teeth chattering a little.

"Of course," Jarrod said, climbing to his feet and hauling Bastian up beside him. "Put this on, you need it way more than I do at this point."

"But—" Bastian began, intending to protest when Jarrod cut him off, not with words, but by wrapping his warm jacket around Bastian's shoulders and following it up by wrapping the blanket and then his arm around him too. God that was so much better. Sighing contently, Bastian let Jarrod escort him back inside where it was warm and the fireplace in the lobby was crackling.

"Wouldn't it be amazing to have one in every room?" Bastian muttered as they crossed through the lobby to get to the elevators.

"Until someone tried to make s'mores and accidently set the room on fire."

Snickering, Bastian found it impossible to ignore the image that had suddenly popped into his head.

"Uh-huh, something tells me that visual mind of yours just conjured up something."

"Yup."

"Care to share?"

"Just…you know how some people are so careful with their marshmallows when they're toasting them," Bastian began as they waited for the elevator, "and others just plunge them into the fire and watch them char?"

"Sure do."

"Now picture a flaming marshmallow sailing across the room 'cause someone yanked it from the fireplace and started shaking it to put the fire out."

Jarrod's laughter consisted of deep, rolling chuckles and the occasional snort. Each time he glanced Bastian's way he only laughed harder, the bright smile on his face leaving Bastian with a feeling of pride that he'd been the one to put it there.

"I love the way you think," Jarrod remarked as they stepped out onto his floor. "Every time I open the curtains now, I'm going to picture that and I'm gonna laugh all over again."

"Funny, the one thing it's got me thinking about is grabbing a bag of marshmallows and bringing them with me to the lobby in the morning so I can have a little snack before my run, though something tells me I'd get some strange looks, and probably a reprimand, if I were to actually go through with it."

"True, but I tell you what, how about a compromise, because I haven't had s'mores in years and the more we talk about them, the more I want to make a batch of fudge stripped ones and savor them while enjoying the campfire smell."

"Fudge stripped s'mores?"

"Don't tell me you've never had them."

"Nope."

"Oh well, then you're in for a treat," Jarrod said. "All we have to do is get a container of fudge striped cookies, a bag of marshmallows and a couple sticks and we'll be all set."

"Aren't you forgetting one big part?"

"What's that?"

"We can't just make s'mores in the fireplace, can we?"

"Nope, but there's a park with a campground not too far from here," Jarrod said. "It's right on the edge of the lake too, so we could take a canoe and row down to it. They've got a self-serve firewood wagon, so that wouldn't be an issue. As long as it's not windy we'd be all set."

"Too bad neither of us has a tent and some sleeping bags, or we could spend the night out there."

"True, though this time of year, with the way the temperature has been dropping, we might be more comfortable with four walls and a thermostat."

Something dawned on Bastian, and he giggled a little. "You sleep with the heat on, don't you?"

"Yeah, don't you?"

"Nope, I can't sleep if it's too warm. Most nights I don't even bother with blankets, just drape a sheet across me and leave my feet sticking out."

"That's going to make things interesting," Jarrod muttered, almost too low for Bastian to hear. He was about to ask what he meant by it when they reached the room and Jarrod slid the card to let them in. A well-organized space, everything had its place, either hung or neatly folded. Jarrod unwound the blanket from him while Bastian glanced around the room, eyes landing on a whip and a riding crop resting on the table.

Jarrod's chuckle was so close it tickled his ear, and he turned to see the man's face inches from his, Jarrod's eyes a stunning ocean blue.

"You've got to oil them periodically to keep them working their best," Jarrod explained.

"Is that to keep them flexible enough that they deliver just the right kind of sting?"

"Yup. You want to keep the leather supple, so it doesn't crack or split. Bad leather can hurt someone and make for an unpleasant experience, which is the last thing I want."

"I've always wondered what they feel like, well, on more than just my hand anyway."

"Oh really?"

Bastian nodded, unable to take his eyes off the things. "Do you use them on the ponies you train?"

"No. Those I carried with me in case I found someone I wanted to play with."

"Oh."

"Would you like me to bring them to play night?"

"I um…I dunno…maybe?"

"Or we could always try them out in private, if you'd like. It doesn't have to be tonight. They'll be there whenever you're ready."

"That'd be cool. I um, think I owe you an answer first."

"Yes, you do, so why don't we get comfortable?" Jarrod said, gesturing to the bed, a large king that dominated the room.

Bastian sprawled across it, joined several minutes later by Jarrod, once he'd adjusted the thermostat and fiddled with something on the bedside table so that the sound of a guitar filled the room. It was mellow, perfect for this time of night, acoustic, and accompanied by a soothing, melodic voice.

"You don't mind, do you?" Jarrod asked.

"No, I like it," Bastian said, content to sink into the softness of the bed as Jarrod draped an arm over him. "Who is it?"

"Eddie Vedder, but that wasn't the question I was asking."

"Oh…umm…"

"You don't mind if I wrap an arm around you, do you?" Jarrod asked, spooning up behind him. "In this position it makes it easier to hold your hand."

Even as he said it, he was seeking Bastian's fingers with his own. To show that he didn't mind in the slightest, Bastian captured his hand and held it close to his body, snuggling into the embrace. Bastian felt Jarrod nuzzle the back of his neck, his breath tickling a little.

"I really do like snuggles," Bastian said. "A lot, actually, especially at the end of the day when everything is getting soft and hazy."

"We had a full day, didn't we?"

"Uh-huh. It was perfect."

"You sound like you're getting sleepy."

"A little. This is nice. Thanks for turning the air on."

"Just wanted you to be comfortable."

"Thank you."

Bastian listened as the song rolled through the room, Vedder's voice crooning about wishing the past would disappear. Bastian knew he could make that happen simply by letting go of the bullshit with Claude. Here was a chance to start something the right way and tell someone he was already very attracted to exactly what he'd come up to the *Pet Play by the Lake* event to find.

"I know that to some people, Master and Daddy are interchangeable, but they aren't to me," Bastian began, choosing his words carefully. "I don't like the word Trainer either, sorry, I just, it makes me feel all prickly and gross, like I need to be fixed or something. I like Keeper though, and Daddy is okay, though I've never had someone in my life that I wanted to call that."

Jarrod gave him a gentle squeeze, his breath soft against Bastian's shoulder and the back of his neck. "Names are what we make of them. They change over time as relationships evolve. I'd find it uncomfortable to have someone call me Daddy or Master right off the bat, especially knowing I hadn't earned the honorarium yet. Things like that take time, and people who insist on it from the beginning are usually those who have some ego issues they need to work out. At least that's been my experience."

"Mine too."

"It seems like you're stalling though. Can I ask why?"

Bastian gave his hand a tiny squeeze even as he inched backward until you couldn't have slipped a piece of paper between them. "I guess it's because I'm still working shit out in my head."

"That's okay."

"I can't figure out if I want too much, or if I'm being reasonable."

"You won't know until you ask."

"True."

When Bastian still didn't say anything, Jarrod gave him a tiny squeeze, then patiently waited him out. It was nice not to be badgered while he worked out what he wanted to say. He could enjoy the music and being held without listening to a long litany of complaints about how long it was taking him to answer a simple question that really wasn't so simple to him.

What *was* simple was how much he enjoyed spending time with Jarrod, and how many things he was curious to explore with him.

"What I really want is someone who'll play with me," Bastian said softly, only to have the moment bolstered by another gentle hug. "I don't want a Keeper who just watches from the sidelines or rolls a ball my way every now and again. I want someone who'll have fun with me. Someone who will chase me through the tunnels or roll over top of them with me. I want someone who doesn't mind climbing, swinging, jumping, and scampering about but can still keep things safe and controlled for me, so I can get lost in it without getting hurt, or accidentally hurting someone. I want someone who will encourage me to have a good time and is okay with me not wanting to curl up on their lap until I'm done. I'll get there, I promise I will, like today."

"You just need to get all worn out first, so your thoughts settle down and your body relaxes, that way you won't get squirmy."

"Yeah," Bastian murmured, feeling hopeful that Jarrod actually got what he was trying to say. "I'd love to have a Keeper who'd enjoy building obstacle courses with me in some corner of the playroom and would take the time to help me get it just right."

"Do you enjoy playing with other pets too?"

"Uh-huh, but mostly just the ones who are rowdy like me," Bastian admitted.

"I can see that, and it doesn't bother me either. Working with the ponies is interactive, what you're describing is pretty much the same thing."

"I do like the brushing and the bows. I love getting dressed up in hats and sweaters and other cute outfits too, especially during the holidays. I have this awesome stocking cap with a snowman face on it, the pom on the top is actually its carrot nose. I have a Halloween costume too, it's a cape and wizard's hat. Dress up parties are my favorites, and I love movie nights, but I have to wear myself out before I go. It's the same way with the movie theater or any event where you're supposed to be sitting the whole time."

Bastian shivered when Jarrod's chuckle sent electric tingles down the back of his neck.

"So what you're saying is, you need to have a bit of playtime before your playtime," Jarrod murmured. "No worries, I am just the kind of Keeper that can manage that."

Chapter 8
When you realize what's lacking

How was he falling so quickly?

On his laptop screen, three adorable ferrets chased one another around a maze made of plastic tubes, ramps, and mini hammocks. He could see it clearly now, how Bastian's parkour and their antics reflected the same carefree spirit. What he hadn't known, until he really sat down and thought about it, was how much he needed that in his life.

He was thirty-six years old, for fuck's sake, not even middle aged yet, but when he looked at his days, the images that flashed behind his eyes were ones of meetings, paperwork, filing petitions and filling out grant applications. It was important work, but somewhere along the line he'd forgotten about living. These past two years, this event had been his one break from all of that, though last year, he'd spent much of the time when he wasn't working with the ponies, holed up in his room, working on details for a huge fundraising event they'd been planning at work.

He'd had something similar planned for this year, only he'd spied Bastian, and his focus had shifted in a most pleasant way. There was no denying the fact that five hours of highway would lay between them once this event was over and they'd returned home. He could deal with that, driving always gave him plenty of time to brainstorm and if he was feeling impatient, it was a short flight from Billingham to Spokane.

The question that remained unasked, was if that would be something Bastian would want, or if he intended for their time together to end once the event was over. The more he thought about it, the less he wanted to see that happened. Determined to show Bastian just what kind of Keeper he could be, Jarrod shot him a text, inviting him to accompany him into town that afternoon.

He'd originally intended to go alone and maybe pick up a few more surprises for the man he was hoping to make his pet. Getting to spend the day in his company would be a bonus, and who knew what they might discover about one another when they were out and about. Damn, were those butterflies fluttering in his stomach when he read Bastian's return text, telling him he'd love to and asking when Jarrod wished to leave?

The sooner the better.

In that case, I'll meet you in the lobby.

Giddy. Excited. Anticipation flooded him as he closed the laptop and stood, looking around for his wallet and shoes. He checked his hair in the mirror and realized he'd forgotten to brush it after his shower. It had finally grown long enough that the ends were beginning to curl. A little gel on his hands before running his fingers through it, and he was ready to go.

Shit.

He looked down at the cutoff sweatpants and rumpled t-shirt he wore, with its faded logo and three holes, and laughed at himself. In his impatience, he'd almost gone down to the lobby in his lounge around clothes. A quick detour to the closet fixed that, and soon he was rushing to the lobby in black jeans and a blue button-down shirt, the sleeves rolled up enough to show off his biceps.

Vein, perhaps, but they were one of his best features, and someone like Bastian, with such a rigorous workout routine of his own, was sure to appreciate them.

Stop trying so hard. He already enjoys spending time with you. If he didn't, he wouldn't have replied so fast, or agreed to join you in the first place.

His inner voice chided him during the duration of the elevator ride, whispering words of caution in his mind, reminding him of all the fun he and Bastian had already had, just hanging out and talking to one another. That's all today needed to be. Another feeling out period. Another opportunity to share more of who he was and get to learn more about Bastian in return. He'd already gotten a glimpse of the man's sense of adventure during their conversation on the lake. Now he had the chance to explore town with him. Who knew what they might encounter.

"Hey," Bastian said, falling in step with him the moment he'd rounded the corner into that bright, spacious entryway.

His hair was worn loose today, rather than back in the short pony tail he tended to wear it in. The moment the sun hit the strands, the colors shimmered, every hue of gold and red standing out now that it wasn't soaked with water or sweat. It was longer than Jarrod had expected it to be, brushing the tops of Bastian's shoulders. Curlier too, sporting a perpetually wind-blown look that framed his face beautifully. It was going to take effort to keep his eyes on the road and not the beautiful man who'd be sitting beside him in his Jeep Wrangler.

"How was your run?" Jarrod asked as they crossed the parking lot.

"Amazing. I took the path along the lake this morning and saw another eagle. This one was circling high above a tree with a fish in its claws. I swear it was singing its own praises, with the way it was calling out while it flew."

"Who knows, it could have been."

At the Jeep he reached to open the door for Bastian, who shot a startled look his way when Jarrod's hand closed over his on the door handle. It was clear that he didn't know what to make of the gesture, even as he withdrew his hand and allowed Jarrod to open it. Still, he didn't protest, or even make a smart remark when Jarrod waited until he was seated to close the door. In fact, his cheeks pinked up a little and his murmured *thanks* was impossible to miss.

"This is nice," Bastian commented as he put his seatbelt on.

The Wrangler had been wistful thinking on his part, but he didn't want to tell Bastian that. "Thanks. I keep meaning to give her a real run for her money, but unfortunately, all she's seen so far are city miles."

"That's a shame."

"Tell me about it. You should load her up with fishing gear and take her into the mountains sometime," Bastian said, his enthusiasm impossible to miss. "That is, um, if you want to."

"Oh, I do," Jarrod said. "I can't believe I haven't made time for it, but I'm starting to realize that I haven't made time for a lot of things in my life that I truly enjoy. Maybe if I had someone just as excited about going, I'd make it a point to arrange a trip."

He made sure to shoot Bastian a pointed look, so there would be no mistake that it was him that Jarrod was talking about.

"I'd be game for that." Bastian replied, clearly getting the hint.

"Good, then we'll have to figure out how to fit it into our schedules. Do you have gear?"

"Yeah. My Gramps made sure of it. He even hooked me up with a cast iron pan perfect for cooking over an open fire with."

"Really?" Jarrod remarked as he put the Jeep in gear. "How often has it gotten used?"

"Not as much as I'd like it to," Bastian admitted. "Though I did make a killer steak and broccoli in mushroom gravy one night when I went camping up at Lake Coeur D'alene. Talk about a beautiful location. I had a hard time leaving when the weekend was over."

"I'll bet."

"I keep meaning to go more often, but then I get caught up in a project, which winds up leading to another one, and the next thing I know, I've wasted the warm months and the snow is flying again."

"Easy enough to do when you love your work."

"Yeah. That is something I've always been grateful for," Bastian admitted. "It's easy to get out of bed and be excited about something when you love what the day has in store for you."

"That is something I can agree on one hundred percent."

They rounded a corner to see a flock of birds on the side of the road, pecking at something and holding court. The moment the Jeep approached all of them took off save for the one closest to the edge of the road. He just stood there and craned his neck, looking back over his shoulder at them like they'd just interrupted a daily planning session. Perhaps they had. Jarrod was just about to make a comment when Bastian let out a bark of laughter.

"What?"

"Did you see that bird back there?" Bastian asked. "The one that didn't take off?"

"Yeah, he looked a little perturbed."

"Seriously. And a bit ruffled too. I might have to sketch that when we get back. It would make an amusing cartoon skit for my website."

"You never said you did cartoons along with your graphic design work."

"That's because I don't do them very often," Bastian admitted. "At least, not the way I used to. That bird though…"

He was laughing again. Like there was some joke Jarrod had missed. One he desperately wanted in on.

"Okay, you can't just sit there and laugh like that without sharing what is going on in your head."

Bastian's chuckles slowed, but it took a few seconds for them to stop completely. "I'm going to draw him with one of those old school leather jackets and a cigarette hanging out of his beak."

"Really, and why is that?"

"Because he seemed really cool and unflappable," Bastian admitted. "We came so close to him that the wind from the car got his tail feathers flapping, but he still didn't twitch. Now all I can see in my head is him standing there when the other birds come back, tail feathers twisted up, maybe a couple are broken and missing. Maybe there's even smoke rolling off a couple of them and yet he's not doing anything about it, he's just standing in that same spot and when they ask about his feathers, he'd just like, mind your business, there's nothing to see here. Like it didn't phase him that he could have been run down."

Snorting, Jarrod couldn't deny the amusement to be found in that impromptu skit. "You have an amazing mind."

Like when he'd opened the door for him, Bastian shot him a look like he didn't understand where Jarrod was coming from, or at the very least, wasn't used to be people valuing him.

"Of course, he could have been so startled he just froze," Bastian admitted, his voice dipping low and a bit whimsical, like he was deep in thought. "Maybe he needed a run coach."

"A what?"

"You know. Someone who tells you when to run and where to run and how fast to run," Bastian explained like it was the most common thing in the world. "All the other birds took off like they already knew what to do. It's like when you're at the mall and people start running. If I see that, I'm running too. I'll figure out why we were all running later. If some massive gator just stormed through the glass doors looking to eat everyone, I don't want to wait around to see it before I get the hell out of the way."

Sputtering, Jarrod guided the Jeep along the road. "Maybe you could draw both?"

"Maybe. I've got everything I need back at my room. Pencils, a sketch pad, I can do a whole mockup here, then use my drawing tablet when I get back home."

"Just promise me one thing," Jarrod requested.

"What's that?"

"That I get a signed copy of the final version when you're through."

"Seriously?"

"I am dead serious about that request," Jarrod insisted. "I plan to frame it and hang it on my wall. I'm going to tell anyone who asks about it that I know the artist too and was in the vehicle when he came up with the idea."

Bastian's cheeks were red when Jarrod glanced over at him, but he had a bright smile on his face and looked positively thrilled. Jarrod loved knowing that he'd put that look on Bastian's face. He knew the perfect spot for the cartoon to be displayed too. Right in his living room, to the left of the television, where he'd be sure to pass by it every day.

"You know, you are always welcome to bring your art supplies up to my room if you want to spend an afternoon lounging, drawing and listening to music," Jarrod offered.

"Won't you be bored watching me draw?"

"Nope. Something tells me that I could never be bored in your presence. Besides, I have a few projects of my own that I really should see to. At least if we were in the same room, we'd still be together, even if we were hard at work."

Silence from Bastian meant contemplation, which told Jarrod that he was at least considering the idea, so he turned on the radio but kept the volume low, so they wouldn't have to yell over it to have a conversation.

"I think that could be fun," Bastian said as the town finally came into view.

Jarrod parked down the block from the pet store, in the first free stop they came too, which happened to sit in front of a shop with stained glass images and dangling prisms hanging in the window. Bastian's eyes lit up as his fingers fumbled for the seatbelt. Before Jarrod could tell him to hang on, and get the door for him, Bastian was out like a shot and headed for the shop, barely managing to shut the door behind him.

His enthusiasm was infectious though. Jarrod followed, stepping into a room of bright colors and delicate pieces of glass covering almost every surface.

"Whoa," Jarrod breathed, struggling to take it all in while still trying to spot Bastian. He hadn't made it far. He stood at a shelf covered in ornate kaleidoscopes, fingers hovering in the air but not touching anything.

"See something you like?" Jarrod asked as he stepped up beside Bastian, who nodded, tongue poking from between his lips.

"All of them. I've never seen anything like this. I don't even know where to look. It's a little overwhelming," Bastian admitted. "There's a big bay window at the front of my apartment where I keep all my succulent plants. There's nothing else in it but them. I think I'd like to hang something there that will throw colors on the wall."

"The first time I heard about those plants, I thought they were called succubus plants," Jarrod admitted, feeling a bit sheepish to say that aloud to someone. "You should have seen the look on the florists face when I asked about them."

Bastian snickered and looked up at him, but nothing could have prepared Jarrod for what he said next. "Same! Oh my god. I love it. I'm glad I'm not the only one. I didn't just say it to the guy in the garden shop either. I asked my grandmother about them. I wanted a plant I wouldn't be able to kill, and I knew she had some. Once she was done laughing and cautioning me that I might want an incubus instead, she hooked me up with a few cuttings off her plants and some lessons in how to tend them."

"Wait…your grandmother…"

"Yeah, she knew the difference, enough to make a joke about it too," Bastian said, cheeks as red as one of the kaleidoscopes that sat on the shelf beside them.

"Okay. I don't feel so bad now at all."

"Thanks." His deadpanned voice didn't match the grin that was still lighting up his face and Jarrod found himself trilled that they'd stopped in there, despite it not being on the list of places he'd planned to check out. Maybe forgetting about the list might be the best way to go for the day.

After some browsing, Bastian bought four prisms, each attached to a strand of blue and purple beads made of shimmering glass. He bought a kaleidoscope too, a purple one with big flakes of purple, silver, and aqua glitter in a glass strand, leaving Jarrod certain he'd already been treated to yet another new bit of knowledge. Bastian's favorite colors.

Jarrod picked up a few pieces for his home as well. Stained glass images of a blue heron by the water's edge and another of an eagle in flight, both reminders of their time on the lake.

They tucked their packages in the back of the Jeep before heading up the block, the backs of their hands bumping a few times before Bastian caught his and raised it a little.

"Is this okay?" he asked, giving Jarrod's hand a gentle squeeze.

"Perfect."

They were still holding hands as they stepped into the pet shop, bright tropical fish in rows of brightly lit tanks the first things that greeted them.

"Do you have fish, too?" Bastian asked as they paused in front of a display of Mollys.

"I do."

"Like these?"

"Yes. Speckled molly fish, actually," Jarrod admitted. "I'm always on the lookout for new display pieces for their tanks. I like to set up themes, especially for the holidays."

"Oh wow, I bet that's awesome."

"They are. Whenever I need to take a break from thinking, I sit in front of their tank and watch them swim."

"I like to do that when I visit the koi ponds. The silvers are always my favorites. I guess because they make me think of ghost fish."

"Have you ever seen the real ones?"

"I didn't even know there were real ones."

"Yup. They're rare, kind of creepy but very beautiful. I saw a few when I visited the aquarium in Seattle."

"I've never been."

"You should check it out, if you're ever in the city."

"I think I might."

Jarrod found a mushroom house, complete with gnomes in the doors and windows. It had a sort of whimsical appeal to it, as did a mushroom capped ice cream shop and couple of happy looking snails that he couldn't resist picking up. He wasn't certain what kind of display he'd create with them yet, but he liked them enough that he put them in his basket, along with a wavy mushroom with grinning facial features that make it look like it had too much to drink. By the time Bastian turned to him with a glow in the dark display of several mushrooms attached to a black rock, he was well on his way to creating his newest theme.

Passing the cages at the back of the shop was inevitable, displays of hamsters, gerbils and mice drew glances from Bastian, but it was the pair of ferrets that held him entranced.

"I don't suppose you have one?" Jarrod asked.

"I've thought about it, but I can't modify the walls of the apartment the way I'd want for them to have a proper play space," Bastian admitted. "I've made a vision board though. It'll be awesome when I can make it happen."

"Do you have names picked out too?"

When Bastian gave a little shrug and licked his lips, Jarrod knew that he did, indeed have some ready and waiting for when he could have some furry friends of his own. It also left him wondering about something else, too. Something he'd been dying to find out.

"If you won't tell me, will you at least tell me what you like to be called when you're in your ferret headspace?" Jarrod leaned in and whispered.

To that, Bastian nodded, and locked eyes with him. "Fergie."

"Fergie Ferret. I love that for you."

"Really?"

"Uh-huh. I can just picture my Fergie in a flurry of motion, bounding everywhere, getting into everything, climbing me when I'm not paying him enough attention and making those adorable little babber, babber sounds."

Bastian leaned in, and at first it seemed to Jarrod like he might kiss him right there in the store. Instead, he brushed his lips over Jarrod's ear and whispered babber, babber babber right in Jarrod's ear. His breath sent a shiver down Jarrod's spine and made the crotch of his pants start to feel just a little bit tight.

"You like the idea of that, don't you?" Jarrod whispered.

Bastian sported a wicked grin when he nodded his response.

"Then we'll need to do all we can to make that happen."

Chapter 9
The warmth of bubbling water

Casual touches. The dance of Jarrod's fingertips down his spine as they stepped into a room together. Hell, the man held doors for him and had even pulled out his chair when they'd gone out to eat. It wasn't even a fancy place they'd stopped for lunch at either. Just a fish house along the lakeside docks. That was three days ago.

In that time they'd learned that they could share silences that weren't really silences while they worked. The music they alternated in choosing wasn't necessarily the same genre, but it complemented the other's choices just the same.

How Jarrod had managed to purchase the bright, colorful balls they'd been playing with all afternoon without Bastian noticing was still a thing that boggled his mind. He loved them though. One squeaked, one rattled and one lit up whenever it bumped into something. Bastian loved that one the best. He'd chased it around the room each time Jarrod rolled it, the blankets on the floor keeping his knees from getting scraped up by the carpet.

It had been easy sinking into his ferret headspace while they'd played their little game of fetch and retrieve. Around the bed, over the bed, wiggling up and over Jarrod when he'd tried to play keep away with the ball, it had all been so light, just playful and fun. No expectations or demands that left Bastian too focused on them to simply enjoy the moment. Now he lay with his head on Jarrod's knee as the Pony Master stroked his hair and gently removed the ears Bastian had happily donned almost two hours before. Jarrod rubbed lazy circles down his back and over his rear before unpinning his tail and laying it next to his ears.

"That was fun," Bastian breathed, relaxed and completely at ease.

"Yes, it was."

"I think I'd totally be up for lounging around the hot tub now."

"You think so?"

"I do, as long as we had it all to ourselves anyway."

Jarrod glanced over to see the glaring red numbers on the clock reading 1:27. "At this time of night, it's a safe bet that we would."

"In that case, we should go."

"That's all well and good, but I'd need you to move first."

"Oh yeah."

"Yup."

When Bastian still didn't move, Jarrod leaned over and kissed the top of his head. "We could always put it off until another time."

"Naa, I'm moving."

"You could have fooled me."

Bastian chuckled, but this time, he did make an effort to sit up. When he grinned and stuck out his tongue at Jarrod, the pony Master leaned in and kissed him, silencing the smartassed remark that had popped into Bastian's head.

His Keeper, 'cause that was how Bastian was rapidly coming to think of Jarrod, framed his face with his hands and peered into his eyes when they broke their kiss. How could he have ever thought Claude was anything but a pretender? He'd have to chalk it up to inexperience and leave the man in the past, because Jarrod was quickly schooling him on what real men did when they cared about someone.

This time, it was Bastian who kissed him, their tongues gliding against one another's, a slow, sensual exploration that was punctuated by light nips and the feel of Jarrod's fingers carding through his hair.

"How about you grab the towels, and I'll grab us a snack to enjoy while we're down there," Jarrod offered, but he didn't let go or break eye-contact.

"Now whose forgetting to move?" Bastian teased.

"More like I forgot how," Jarrod said before leaning in and kissing him again. This time, he found himself hauled against Jarrod's chest as the man sprawled backwards on the floor and pulled Bastian with him.

Soft caresses. The press of warm flesh against his side and hip. He was well aware of the skimpiness of his boy shorts, and the rough contrast of Jarrod's jeans. They made out in a slow, unhurried manner, the clock reading three minutes to two before either of them came up for air again.

"We keep this up and it's a cold tub we'll be needing," Jarrod murmured against his lips.

"I guess that means you'll have to let me up or help me find one."

"Decisions, decisions."

In the end, Jarrod did let go, so Bastian slid off him carefully and took a moment to sit on the floor, savoring the aftermath of those decadent kisses.

"How is it you always have a stash of treats stocked up in your refrigerator?" Bastian asked as Jarrod retrieved a carton from the freezer section.

"Seemed like a good idea, after the way you enjoyed our impromptu breakfast picnic."

With anyone else, Bastian might have cracked off a joke, or made a comment about them assuming he had a love affair with food, but with Jarrod, it felt unnecessary. The man seemed to genuinely enjoy keeping things around to surprise him with.

He didn't ask what it was. If it was anything like the contents of the picnic basket Jarrod had packed for their trip out onto the lake, he'd make sure Bastian was left guessing right up until that moment Jarrod popped something into his mouth.

Energized by the thought of another snack nibbled off Jarrod's fingers, and more kisses if he played his cards right, Bastian climbed to his feet and went in search of the towels and the pair of slides he'd worn earlier that night.

"All set?" Jarrod asked. He'd slipped out of his jeans and into swim shorts. Now he stood waiting for Bastian by the door.

"You've got your room key, right?" Bastian asked, not wanting a repeat of the incidents with Chauncy.

"Right here," Jarrod remarked, holding it up for Bastian to see. In his other hand, he held the snack he'd pulled from the freezer, conveniently kept just out of view.

At this time of night the lodge was silent. Jarrod led him out to one of several outdoor hot tubs located just behind the glassed-in pool. There were even partitions set up between each one, not that any of them were occupied.

"I didn't even know these were out here," Bastian admitted. "I thought we were going to the inside one beside the pool."

"We could if you want, but the more I thought about it, the better these seemed. The water will keep us warm enough, and we have an unobstructed view of the stars."

"No, this is perfect."

It was, too. The air had a nip in it, but as soon as Jarrod got the jets going and they slid into the water, things started heating up. Soon, he was reclined back with his head pillowed against one of Jarrod's arms, a brilliant blanket of stars glittering overhead.

"Did you ever wish on the first star of the night when you were a kid?" Bastian asked.

"Doesn't everyone?"

"I thought so," Bastian admitted. "Then I asked Chauncy if he ever had, and he asked what the point would have been in making wishes when all he had to do was ask his old man for something and it was his."

"That's a shame. All kids should believe in wishes."

"Yeah."

Bastian cuddled closer, turning his head so he could press a kiss against Jarrod's neck. One kiss wasn't enough though, so Bastian did it again, turning so he could straddle

Jarrod's lap and kiss him properly. Even with the bubbles churning up the water around them, Bastian could feel how happy Jarrod was to have him perched on him. The slow, lazy kisses of earlier grew in demand, until their tongues were engaged in a hot and heavy duel.

"Tell me about them," Jarrod asked when they'd finally broken apart.

Blinking, Bastion could only stare down at him and wonder what the hell Jarrod was talking about. Jarrod chuckled and the next thing Bastian knew, Jarrod was gently booping him on the nose.

"Focus."

"I was," Bastian grumbled, doing his best to glare, only Jarrod was smiling, which meant the best Bastian could manage was to bite back a grin of his own.

"I asked you what you wished for," Jarrod said as he carded his fingers through Bastian's hair.

"All the usual kids' stuff," Bastian admitted. "A puppy, a toy, to go white water rafting, that kind of thing. The rafting my uncles and I did. The puppy was always a no go because my mom was allergic."

"That sucks."

"Tell me about it. Sometimes I'd wish for my own room. Or for school to be canceled the next day so I could stay home and draw. Once I wished for the car to break down. We'd stopped in this town with an old arcade, and I really wanted to check it out, but my old man said we didn't have time. I'm pretty sure I heard one of my brothers wish for the same thing."

Jarrod chuckled at that and tugged Bastian into a gentle kiss.

"What about you?" Bastian asked.

"Pretty similar. I tried wishing for a younger sibling for a while, and that my parents would get a VW bug, one of the old classic ones. I don't know why I was so obsessed with them, but for about three years that was one of my top wishes."

"Oh man, my brothers and I would play the punch buggy game on every family trip. My mom would get so mad because eventually somebody would hit someone too hard and a squabble would break out, especially if someone got hit more than once."

"We'd always play the license plate game," Jarrod told him. "Mom would write down every state that was called out, and whoever had called out the most states by the end of the trip got an extra dessert."

"Ohh nice."

"I know, right," Jarrod said as he reached for the container he'd sat just on the other side of the towels. Of course, the fluffiness of them had obscured Bastian's view of the label the entire time they were in the tub. "Speaking of dessert, you know the drill."

Giggling, Bastian closed his eyes and parted his lips a little, waiting for the feel of this latest treat to be pressed against them.

It was the scent that hit him first. Chocolate. He flicked out his tongue and felt the cold confection brush against it before it was withdrawn, replaced by Jarrod's lips. He melted into a kiss that tasted as chocolaty as the treat Jarrod had teased him with. So sweet and enticing. Jarrod broke the kiss, only to brush the chocolate over his lips again. This time, Bastian parted them more, and Jarrod popped it into his mouth.

For a moment, he rolled it around on his tongue, until the chocolate started melting and a second burst of flavors sent a burst of pleasure through his taste buds.

"Mmmmmm," he sighed at the first hint of cherry-vanilla ice cream.

"It sounds like someone approves," Jarrod murmured, sounding quite pleased with himself.

Bastian took his time savoring the treat, discovering a third layer, the cherry in the center, before replying. "They're my favorites, but I've never had them like that before."

Jarrod's chuckle was as sweet and tantalizing as the treats he shared, but it didn't seem fair to Bastian that he got to have all the fun. Reaching past him, he managed to get his fingers in the carton, enough to pluck one from the container, so he could hold it to Jarrod's lips. Of course, Jarrod turned the tables on him, taking it from Bastian, who tried to protest, only to find his mouth filled with another of those delectable bon-bons.

"Not fair," he tried to saw around the melty confection in his mouth, but it just came out rumbly and unintelligible. Jarrod clearly got the gist of it though, because he laughed and rubbed noses with him.

Their gazes locked and that's when Jarrod whispered. "I say what's fair or not."

Bastian's spine felt like it was liquifying right along with the ice cream that melted in his mouth. He shivered, swallowed, and kissed Jarrod with the type of wild inhibition he typically reserved for his morning runs.

How could he convey everything he was feeling. Safe, protected, cared for but not confined. Even when he was taking control, Jarrod was giving something in return, and that was the sort of exchange Bastian could appreciate.

Jarrod's hands skimmed up his thighs before settling on his hips, firm, possessive, clinging to him while Bastian rocked in his lap, a teasing dance that excited them both. Fingers closed in his hair, and Bastian found his head tugged backwards, exposing his throat to Jarrod's lips and tongue. Before long, he started involving teeth. The gentlest little nips over Bastian's collarbone and shoulder, each one punctuated by a tiny pinprick of deliciously sharp pleasure.

Jarrod's blue eyes reflected the lights of the hot tub, when Bastian could next focus on them. His cheeks were flushed, though Bastian doubted it was the heat of the tub that had left them that way. He could have stayed like that forever, studying the flecks of color in Jarrod's gaze. It was like the place where the sky met the ocean, the blues clashing and blurring together, all glittering beneath the light of the sun.

"I don't want to move," Jarrod murmured, tugging Bastian to him for a gentle kiss this time. "If wishes were real, I'd wish for time to freeze us here forever, or at the very least, wrap a big glass dome around us to keep the rest of the world at bay."

"Like the inside of a snow globe," Bastian said.

"Only without the snow."

Giggling, Bastian tilted his head back to see the stars again. The night was clear, with only a few bugs flittering about, attracted by the light of the hot tub. "Warm as it is in here, I wouldn't mind a little bit of swirling snow, as long as it didn't stick."

"That's the problem with wishing for snow," Jarrod said. "It always has a mind of its own."

"True. But imagine if it did come whirling around us. We really would have our own magical snow globe moment then."

"Maybe one day you can use your software to create that image of us."

"True, but we'd need a base picture first."

"I have my phone," Jarrod offered, reaching between the towels to grab it.

Pressed together, they posed for a series of selfies until they finally managed one with enough of the hot tub in the background to make Jarrod's idea work. It would still take some doing to get it just right, but something told him that by the time he'd finished, it would be something he'd never tire of looking at. As it was, he intended to make it his lock screen, so that every time he opened his phone, he could remember this moment and how happy they'd looked.

"Images sent," Jarrod said before returning his phone to its place among the towels.

"Too bad it was the wrong season for a snow globe filter," Bastian said. "Your phone could have done it for us."

"True, but I bet it wouldn't be near as awesome as what you'll create."

"What makes you say that?"

"Just looking at the drawings you sketched out on the napkins while we were waiting for our food."

"You were watching me? I thought you were studying the menu."

"What do you think took me so long to decide what I wanted?"

It felt good to know he'd been able to distract the man that way, especially with something that came so natural to him. Claude used to take the napkins away from him and crumple them up, chide him for being childish, or flat out complain that Bastian was ignoring him. That was never his intention. He just reached for whatever was handy when inspiration hit. It hadn't been long into the relationship with Claude that he'd stopped drawing cartoons altogether, or doing anything fun with his artwork. Spending time with Jarrod was starting to remind him of how much he loved and missed all the fun pieces he used to create. He'd been so excited about the bird cartoon that he hadn't been able to resist creating a mockup of what he had planned. It hadn't dawned on him until now that Jarrod hadn't minded in the slightest.

Everything about Jarrod was a refreshing change. The more time they spent together, the easier it was becoming for Bastian to relax and just be himself. He'd stopped thinking about who and what he wasn't and started to enjoy living spontaneously again.

"You're thinking really hard about something," Jarrod said. "I hope it's something good."

"Oh, it is."

"Are you going to tell me about it, or shall I try to guess?"

"I don't know, listening to you guess might be interesting."

"Well, in that case, I wouldn't want to disappoint you," Jarrod said, tapping a finger to the side of his face. "Let's see. We've already covered hot tub snow globes, and cocky birds who don't know enough to move so they don't get flattened. What direction could that imagination of yours have turned in now? I know. Scuba diving insects."

Jarrod punctuated his response with a snap of his fingers, eyes wide, like he'd just made the greatest discovery in the world. While Bastian struggled to marshal his thoughts and figure out where the hell that answer had come from, Jarrod scooped a waterlogged moth in his hands and deposited it, still floundering, on the stones around the hot tub.

"Pretty sure that poor moth could have used some gear before he went hunting for the lights."

As Bastian studied it, a picture began to form in his head of the moth with scuba gear and a mask on. That seemed a bit much though, so he tried imagining it with a snorkel mask and fins, maybe an over-exaggerated set of antenna and more color on it's wings, though not enough to transform it into a butterfly. It already looked to be doing better, no longer frantically fluttering and staggering around. How many people would have ignored it's plight, or never even noticed it struggling in the first place? Jarrod had though. He was starting to realize that Jarrod noticed a lot of things that other people didn't, especially about him. It felt good to be someone's priority for once, even if it only proved to be for a little while.

"I will draw him snorkeling," Bastian declared. "But only if you'll pull up a few pictures of your aquarium, so I can add your tank and the fish too."

"How do you know that I have any?"

"It just seems logical. Someone who cares enough about their tank to create themed displays for their fish would surely take pictures of them when they were done."

Jarrod laughed and reached for the phone again. "Okay, you got me."

There were more than just a few images on the phone. Jarrod had snapped shots of his fish weaving in and out of a beach themed display, and others of a big speckled molly fish swimming over top of a leprechaun. Everything in that tank was green and gold, including a pot that was spilling over with actual coins. The tank was clean too, the water pristine and beautiful, proving once again that Jarrod took care of the things that belonged to him.

"Thank you," Bastian said, snuggling back in Jarrod's arms as he scrolled through the pictures.

"For what?"

"Making every moment we spend together special."

Jarrod hugged him close and kissed the side of his head. "And to think that I've only just begun."

Chapter 10
When the magic melts the moment

"Wow. You're magnificent," Jarrod murmured as he leaned in low to brush a kiss on Bastian's cheek. His pet was sprawled naked across his bed, warm, drowsy, and fresh from their latest soak in the hot tub downstairs. For the past four days, it had become a daily ritual.

"I'm not doin' anything."

"You don't have to be. Just the sight of you lying there is enough for me. Besides, I told you I had something for you, and you are in the perfect position to receive it."

"Yeah, what's that?"

"Now, if I told you, how would it be a surprise?" Jarrod asked, ruffling his hair before turning his back to the bed. What he was after was in his bag and would take several minutes to set up, not that he was worried about Bastian going anywhere. He was already relaxed and leaving an imprint in the comforter. By the time Jarrod was through with him, he hoped to have him reduced to a puddle of goo.

Tonight the smart speaker was playing Ed Sheeran, a soft glow filling the room from the lamps on either side of the bed. Bastian looked so peaceful with his hair swept to the side and his head pillowed on one arm as he stared off into the distance. Jarrod laid several items out on the bed within easy reach before taking a seat beside him and trailing his fingertips down his back.

"I didn't know he wrote this," Bastian muttered as the smart speaker played the haunting opening of "I See Fire".

"Yup. It's one of my favorites."

"Every time I hear it, I think about the movie, and how the dwarves fought so hard and sacrificed so much to get their home back."

"When something is important enough, no sacrifice is too great," Jarrod said, still lightly stroking his back.

"That final battle was brutal. Talk about amazing cinematography though, the *Lord of the Rings* and *Hobbit* trilogies are some of the best shot movies I've ever seen."

"Same. I love a movie with a gut-wrenching storyline that doesn't need to rely on things blowing up every twelve seconds to keep the audience interested."

"I think that was the biggest issue I had with the Transformer series," Bastian said. "I wanted to love it, 'cause the cartoons were awesome, but after a while, there was just too much destruction and too little in the way of storytelling."

Jarrod nodded as he opened the lid on the first container he picked up. "I tried watching the first movie, but it did nothing for me. I've never been a big fan of robot movies anyway. Too cold and impersonal."

"Same. I prefer fantasy. I love getting lost in all the amazing worlds. *Labyrinth* is one of my favorites, so is *The Dark Crystal* and the *NeverEnding Story*. I love the *Alice in Wonderland* movies too, and *Narnia*. *Avatar* is pretty awesome too."

"I never get tired of that one," Jarrod admitted as he drizzled warming oil across Bastian's back.

"Oh my god, what is that?" Bastian remarked, laughing and squirming. "Holy shit, it tickles."

"Really? And how ticklish are you?"

"Like I'd tell you!"

"Why, worried I might exploit it?"

"Pretty much."

"And what makes you think I won't find all your ticklish spots on my own and exploit them anyway?" Jarrod asked, already dancing his fingers through the slippery oil while Bastian continued to wiggle.

"What are you doing, writing your name?"

"Maybe."

"Mmmm it sure feels like you're writing something."

"I am."

"But you're not going to tell me what, are you?"

"Not yet, anyway. Not when I'm just getting started."

"Hmm I like the sound of that," Bastian admitted, soft sighs seeping from him as Jarrod ran a finger across the back of his neck, tracing a pattern of symbols and letters.

Leaning in, Jarrod blew over the lines he made, chuckling when he drew a gasp and a shiver from Bastian. He kept his movements slow, taking his time to warm each one, soaking up the sounds Bastian made, even while he kept a mental tally of the squirmy, ticklish spots he hit. One thing was certain. Bastian had plenty of them.

Bastian hummed, a soft sigh escaping him. "You keep doing that and I'm not going to be able to move."

"That's the point."

"Ohhh."

The sound was drawn out, low and long, when Jarrod added several lines of cooling gel to his back, making certain to draw through the warm ones for duel sensations. He traced those with his tongue, paying specific attention to the back of Bastian's neck, the edges of his earlobes, and the junctions where his neck met his shoulders.

He kept each touch light, tracing with just the pads of his fingertips, drawing soft sighs from Bastian, whose eyelids looked to grow heavier with every gentle touch. Chuckling, Jarrod reached for surprise number three, eager to see how his new pet would respond to the metal claws he slipped over his fingertips.

The first lazy, serpentine drag across Bastian's shoulders drew a sharp gasp from him, then a whine more whimper than moan. Leaning over him, Jarrod nipped his ear and whispered, "Do you like that?"

"No," Bastian groaned, drawing in a ragged moan, breath hitching when Jarrod danced the claws down his spine. "I l–love it."

This time, when he laughed, he made sure Bastian felt it against the back of his shoulder. He knew the gel he'd applied would leave Bastian's skin extra-sensitive and sure enough, goosebumps pimpled the ridge of his shoulder and continued halfway down his arm.

Jarrod grazed the claws down his side next and was rewarded with a yelp and laughter as Bastian squirmed to get away. A firm hand placed in the center of his pet's back stilled those efforts, and once again Jarrod leaned over him and growled in his ear. "I told you I'd find the ticklish places."

He didn't torment him though, he moved on with the touching, caressing the backs of his legs and finding more spots there, including behind the knees. Never once did Bastian plead with him to stop. He hooted, he giggled, he whined and whimpered and snickered and laughed until a few tears rolled down his cheeks and every touch left him gasping for breath and chuckling.

Only then did Jarrod put the claws away, and only after running them over the bottom of Bastian's foot and watching his pet flop across the bed.

"Not fair," Bastian whined.

"Who said?"

His pet narrowed his eyes, mouth opening and closing without a sound coming out.

"That's what I thought. Now, get back over here. I wasn't done with you yet."

"Are you gonna tickle me some more?" Bastian asked, crossing his arms over his chest and giving his best stubborn look, which just came out a tad petulant and so utterly adorable, Jarrod leaned in and kissed him rather than answer the question. Like in the hot tub, Bastian melted into his arms, slipping forward until he was straddling Jarrod's lap.

Bastian kissed the way he ran out on the trail, wild and uninhibited. He blew Jarrod away with the intensity of it all, and the way he wasn't afraid to tangle his fingers in Jarrod's hair or draw his nails down Jarrod's arms and back. His little pet was certainly not afraid to give as good as he got and that was just one of many things he was coming to discover that he absolutely loved about him. It wasn't long before they were wrapped in each other's arms, bodies rubbing against one another as they writhed on the bed.

By the time they broke apart, they were gasping. Bastian's lips looked a little puffy and red, his eyes glazed and lust filled, and that's when Jarrod knew he was ready for phase two of their little game.

"Close your eyes and keep them closed," Jarrod ordered, growled words low and firm. The shiver they produced, coupled with the newest crop of goosebumps, was more than enough to tell him where his pet's mind was.

Bastian's eyelids fluttered before he finally squeezed them shut, but seconds later, they popped open again, his gaze seeking Jarrod's.

Jarrod cupped his cheek and traced the edge of his jawline. "Do you need a blindfold, or can you behave and do it on your own?"

"You're gonna tickle me again, aren't you?" Bastian muttered, but he was already closing his eyes like the good boy he was.

"Perhaps."

"I can keep them shut," Bastian insisted, pressing his hands over them for good measure.

"Good boy," Jarrod murmured, punctuating it with a kiss to his abs, which clenched, even as his cock bobbed, growing even harder at the sound of Jarrod's words. Well then, he'd just have to add that to the growing list of things he was learning about his pet. A praise kink was something he could certainly feed into. Nothing would make him happier than seeing a pleased flush creep over his pet's body as he let him know how pleased Jarrod was with him. "Such a good, good, boy."

Oh yeah, his little one loved hearing that. He wore an ear-to-ear grin and his cock stood proudly at attention, just begging for a kiss, which Jarrod was happy to reward it with. It drew a little gasp and a small moan from his pet, along with a bead of precum which Jarrod was thrilled to lick away.

Sensitive, responsive, wild, and uninhibited too. He thought nothing of getting naked and staying that way whenever they were in the room together, that first night being the only one in which he'd fallen asleep with clothes on. It was a running joke that they hit the floor now the second the door was closed and didn't go back on until it was time to leave again. Frankly, Jarrod loved it. Not only did it give him a chance to study his pet and memorize every plane and angle of his body, but he'd finally had the opportunity to get up close and personal with that tattoo.

Like now, when he reached for the feather he'd laid out beside his oils, and traced the intricate Celtic wings with them.

"You still haven't told me the story about this," Jarrod said as he carefully used the tip to tickle and taunt. "Why wings? And why lines instead of feathers."

"It's umm…I didn't want anything soft," Bastian replied, another giggle bubbling up from his throat. "I wanted something to remind me of this poem my best friend wrote before he moved away."

"What's it called?"

"*Only Birds and Angels Fly.*"

"Sounds kind of sad, and more than a little bit ominous."

"It was, in a way, I guess. I always found it pretty, even if there were lines about crashing to the ground in a tangle of arms and legs. I always took it as a reminder that exhilaration was fleeting, but we needed to feel it to know we were alive, otherwise we might as well be dead inside. The first line, kinda sums it up really."

"Oh yeah, and what does it say?" Jarrod asked, nearly finished with his feather dance along the lines, having moved from one collarbone to the next, and gotten Bastian to arch up into the feel of that feather's tip.

"I just wanted to fly, I never thought it would hurt like this," Bastian said, his words punctuated with a gasp and moan.

"I think I get it," Jarrod said, giving the feather a rest for a moment. "It's not just about literally flying, it's about the things we long for, and the sometimes painful results."

Bastian stayed silent for a moment, but that smile of his grew and he reached for Jarrod, even as he kept his eyes closed like he'd been told to do. "You really do get it."

"I want to get everything there is to get about you," Jarrod admitted as he slid over top of him and hugged him close. Bastian's content sigh and the sound of his heartbeat as they lay chest to chest, was better than any song the smart speaker could have played. Rolling, Jarrod pulled Bastian on top of him and kissed his head.

He expected questions about whether or not playtime was over, maybe even a protest or two about the direction the evening had turned, but again, his pet surprised him, going with the flow and snuggling into Jarrod's embrace.

"Do you read a lot of poetry?" Jarrod asked, rubbing lazy circles on his back as he held him.

Bastian giggled, his breath tickling Jarrod's shoulder. "I've never read *any*. My friend always read his pieces to me. He'd work on them while I fiddled with some project I was working on."

"I see."

"Sorry if that's disappointing. I've never been a big fan of poetry. The stuff we were forced to read in school was always too hard to connect with. I don't know if it was the way it was composed, or the archaic language, or just that it felt so out of touch, but I could never get into it."

"No worries, neither could I."

"It was easy to connect with his poems though, 'cause they were his and he was sharing a part of himself with me," Bastian admitted. "It's like when someone you care about is really excited about something, and you listen, even when it isn't something you're interested in. It doesn't cost anything to do that for them, and sometimes you get lucky and discover something that resonates with you too."

"Like that poem."

"Yeah, exactly. I hate when people are so wrapped up in themselves that whenever someone tries to tell them about something, they either respond with an *I know*, an *I'm not interested*, or *that's stupid*. There's no reason to yuck someone else's yum just because it's not *your* thing. It's kinda sad, really. I wonder if they ever think about how that friend felt afterward or wondered why that person stopped telling them things."

"Probably not," Jarrod said. "People who do stuff like that are too wrapped up in themselves to see what's going on with anyone else. They're happy to have someone there for them when they need an ear to listen, but when it comes time to reciprocate, it's like it's too much trouble for them to be bothered with."

"That's why I miss Shep so much. We could talk about anything. Lately, with Chauncy, I feel like I'm walking on eggshells. The least little thing seems to set him off."

"That's never a good thing."

"No, it really isn't."

"I hope you know that you can talk about anything with me."

Bastian snuggled deeper into his arms and breathed a single word against his skin. "Thanks."

"Something tells me you really needed to hear that."

"Yeah, but I feel like I killed the fun with all the serious," Bastian admitted. "I could have just said I love Celtic designs and left it at that when you asked about the wings."

"But that wouldn't have been what I wanted to hear."

"Oh."

"The fun will always be there, and for the record, this is fun, just laying here and holding you," Jarrod assured him. "Was I enjoying tormenting you, yes, and I learned plenty of ways to make you squirm. But I also enjoy reaching the heart of you, and that is more rewarding then seeing you flush with pleasure for me."

"Pretty sure I'm flushing now," Bastian muttered.

Jarrod palmed his ass and gave it a little squeeze. "You do feel a little warm."

"That's 'cause you're always saying things to me that make me wonder who you're looking at."

"You," Jarrod assured him. "And trust me when I say I like what I see, even the parts you don't think show."

There was a scar trailing from the curve of Bastian's hip to the small of his back, thin, shiny, and slightly jagged. Jarrod had noticed it when he'd been playing with the oil, now his fingertips encountered it, and he found himself wondering what had caused it. It had the smooth feel of old tissue, and Bastian shivered when he touched it. "What happened here?"

Bastian let out a long sigh before he answered. "Broken lava lamp."

"I thought those things were next to indestructible."

"Don't I wish."

"What happened?"

"A couple of my brothers were roughhousing in our room," Bastian began. "Actually, it was more like Robbie was roughhousing and Mark was his victim like always, not that he didn't bring it on himself by egging Robbie on all the time. I don't know what got them started, just that Robbie caught Mark in a headlock and Mark tried to shove him off, and in the middle of it all, they hit my dresser, and a couple things fell over, including my lava lamp. I'd just gotten the damned thing. It broke and I got pissed, shoved Robbie, who was like, seventy pounds heavier than me and a wrestler, so of course I went flying when he shoved me back. Right into the mess of the lava lamp."

"Ouch."

"Pretty much. Add needing stitches and it just sucked all the way around. I never did get another lava lamp, either. I didn't see the point with those two around."

"Why not after you moved out?"

Bastian sighed and nuzzled the hand Jarrod pressed to the side of his face. "I guess by then it wasn't important."

"So what was?"

"Figuring shit out," Bastian admitted. "The beds at the house were bunk beds, so I couldn't take one with me. I moved out with my clothes, my art supplies, a dresser, and a secondhand computer I'd picked up from a pawn shop. I got lucky with the rooming house, my uncle owned it, so he only charged me twenty-five bucks a week to live there, but I still had to make that in design jobs each month. Plus come up with grocery money. The first few months it was peanut butter and jelly sandwiches, then I got an electric kettle and a couple bowls, which meant I could at least have Ramen."

"What did you do for a bed?"

"Blanket nest," Jarrod replied.

Stroking Bastian's hair, Jarrod couldn't help but think about the kind of grit and determination it took for his pet to work his way up from nothing. "I admire your persistence, lots of people would have moved back home, or given up their dream and taken a job they hated."

"I thought about it, but in the end, I didn't see a point," Bastian said. "I was doing okay. I never missed rent, I never went hungry, and I had privacy for the first time in my life."

"There are some folks who'd say that was barely surviving."

"Maybe for them, for me it was everything."

As he lay holding Bastian in his arms, Jarrod had to ponder how he felt about that. Bastian's words had been spoken with such conviction, but Jarrod was torn. A part of him wondered if Bastian always had such low expectations, and if so, how did that translate to how Bastian saw him? Was he a take what he could get kinda guy, always willing to settle, never seeing his own worth, or did he just have different values and the ability to appreciate simpler things?

Jarrod found himself hoping for the latter. What a refreshing change that would be from some of the self-absorbed pets he'd played with in the past. They'd been fun, but he'd quickly realized they believed the world revolved around them and everything should be to their very specific liking.

Like the impression he'd gotten of Chauncy. How the hell had Bastian wound up with such a friend?

"Can I ask for something?"

Bastian's soft request jarred him from his thoughts, and he opened his eyes to see his pet staring down at him. "You can ask for whatever you'd like."

"It's just...there's something I've been dying to do," Bastian admitted. "You got to do it tonight, and now I'd like to do it too."

"Oh yeah? What's that?"

"Taste you."

"Really?"

"Uh-huh."

"Well now," Jarrod said, carding his fingers through Bastian's hair as he drew out his answer. "I think that can be managed. You deserve a treat and I know I do."

Chapter 11
One wrong spiral changes everything

For the fifth morning in a row, Bastian had woken in Jarrod's arms to soft music playing and the sun barely brightening the sky. He'd given up his morning reading time for an extra hour of snuggling, and reluctantly slipped away for his morning run while the man still slept. Chauncy wasn't particularly thrilled with his new sleeping arrangements, but Bastian had told his friend outright that he was going to spend every free moment he could with Jarrod in order to see where things might go. After all, the event would come to an end far too soon, and he was hopeful that this would turn into something that extended well beyond that.

Of course, the moment Bastian had mentioned that Jarrod lived in Bellingham, Chauncy hadn't been able to resist pointing out how infrequently long-distance relationships worked out in the end, which had prompted Bastian to remind him that any connection they formed here would become long distance in just a few weeks, so it was best to make the most of it. He'd also pointed out that his friend's bitterness and jealousy were beginning to show, again, and that it wasn't a good look on him.

In the end, it had been Chauncy who'd stormed out, tossing a jab over his shoulder about Bastian being an attention whore, to which he'd wound up calling his friend a needy bitch. Distance, he hoped, would mellow his friend out, or else Bastian would be looking for another way home after the event.

Still frustrated with the way the conversation had gone, Bastian leapt onto a bench only to lean too far forward and send himself tumbling over the back. He managed to tuck his head and roll over his shoulders at the very last minute, but there was no popping up from that. He lay there for a moment with the wind knocked out of him, rolled over, brushed the leaves and a few smudges of dirt off his shirt, and took off again.

This wasn't what they'd come here for. They were supposed to be supporting one another, not be at each other's throats, and while he understood Chauncy's frustration, it wasn't fair for his friend to try and take it out on him. Not when Bastian had tried his best to be encouraging and had even asked Jarrod if he knew anyone who might want to play with a kitty, since Chauncy was hell bent on attending tonight's open play event.

He hadn't, but he'd said he'd keep his ears open, though with time ticking down, Bastian couldn't help but feel like

Chauncy would be setting himself up for another lonely evening by showing up there. Somehow, it felt like his friend might try and blame him for that, too, which was the last thing he was in the mood to deal with. Not when everything else about the trip was proving to be as relaxed and wonderful as he'd hoped it would be.

Thanks to Jarrod.

Just picturing the man in his mind was a tad distracting. Those arms, holy shit, there was no doubt they could crush someone if Jarrod had a mind to, but with Bastian he was the perfect mix of gentle and firm.

He mistimed another leap and slammed face first into a hedge like a cartoon coyote, all that was missing was the body shaped imprint. It prickled and stabbed, a tad more painful than his earlier mistake. He knew better than to continue a run when his focus was shot, but stubbornness prevailed and a spiraled springboard off the side of a tree soon had things kicked into high gear again.

A branch hung low over the trail, thick enough that he knew it would support his weight. He did pull ups until a squirrel chattered at him for disturbing it, then he was off again, hopping on a planter and back flipping off.

A sense of joy flowed through him, accompanied by memories of the night before. Jarrod's voice rumbled when he spoke, his cadence low and rolling. It had a soothing quality that Bastian hadn't known he needed until they were laying together watching a movie and Jarrod had actually begun talking to him about it rather than insisting Bastian sit in silence.

They'd laughed with the characters, cheered them on, called them dumbasses and tossed out all kinds of quips about what they'd do if they found themselves in that situation. They'd quickly moved from well thought out and calculating to completely off the wall. When Jarrod tipped headlong into the realm of the bizarre, Bastian found he didn't have to worry about the random, unfiltered thoughts that flew through his head, they were welcome, and even encouraged here.

Tonight, he'd promised that Bastian would get to try the crop for the first time, in the privacy of his room during a little one on one playtime before they headed down to the playroom for the open event. He was glad now that he'd brought two different versions of his gear, the full suit, and one that was simply comprised of ears, a tail, a mask, a bowtie, and a skimpy pair of boy shorts.

Spring boarding off a bench, Bastian spun, intent on hitting the ground running, instead, he smacked something solid and rough, the back of his head, neck, and shoulders scraping down the bark of the tree he hit. A riot of pain shot through him and left him gasping on the grass, the sky above him spinning and filled with dancing spots of gold and gray.

This time he took much longer to pick himself up. Rolling his shoulders and neck, he ensured nothing was hurt too badly, though his head throbbed in time with his heartbeat, which wasn't particularly slow. Groaning, he stayed seated with his back to the tree until his vision cleared. Something tickled his shoulder and he brushed at it, expecting to find a caterpillar or some marauding bug. Instead, his fingers were met with a sticky smear of his own blood.

That was it. Run over. He inched his fingers over the back of his head and encountered a lump already forming. His skin stung where he'd scraped it, and turning his head produced a series of cracks and pops that ran up the side of his sore and aching neck. The first effort he made at getting back to his feet was a failure. He got halfway up and the world spun, leaving him sprawled on his side, but at least he didn't hit the tree again. Close though, and he was certain he'd bruised his side by falling over on the roots.

He waited a bit longer before trying again, and this time he was successful, though he needed a moment of pause once he was back on his feet, to get acclimated. It was a slow walk back to the lodge and he tried not to imagine what people saw when they looked at him. A mess, probably. He didn't want to freak anyone out with the bleeding, though it seemed to have stopped. There was no way to be sure until he got upstairs and looked in the mirror, though with where the damage was, it would be difficult to treat anything. In the elevator, he debated which button to hit, Jarrod's voice creeping into his mind once again.

As long as you understand that playing with you and having fun will always be secondary to my primary concern, which is keeping you safe. Doesn't matter if it's during playtime, out on the water, or right here in this room, I will take care of you, no matter what you need. You just have to be honest with me and not hide things. That's really important to me.

They were supposed to play tonight, something he'd been excited about all week. Would him getting hurt mean their evening would be canceled? He didn't want that. Only, with the way he was feeling right now he wasn't sure if he wanted to roll and climb and do his usual sort of playing either.

When the elevator stopped on Jarrod's floor, he didn't hesitate to get off. It was entirely possible he wouldn't be here and his fretting would be for nothing. Maybe he was reading too much into things. Maybe Jarrod had only meant for him to tell him things when they were together.

Had coming up here been a mistake?"

Shit.

The only way you'll know is to ask.

He knocked with those words echoing in his head, trusting that Jarrod wouldn't be upset with him if he checked in about the accident, 'cause really, he wanted to sit down and once he did, he wasn't sure he'd be going anywhere this evening. The least he could do was explain that he needed to postpone their playtime until he was feeling better.

Of course, he could have waited to do that until he'd gotten back to his room where his phone was…

Before he could give himself a worse headache by continuing the round robin of should he or shouldn't he, the door was pulled open, and there was Jarrod. He went from smiling to serious in an instant, taking in Bastian's appearance and immediately ushering him in.

"How bad did you crash?" Jarrod asked as he led him to the chair beside the table. Bastian hissed, despite the gentleness of the hand Jarrod pressed to his shoulder to urge him to sit down. "Shit, sorry."

"I kinda careened into a tree." Damn it felt good to sit. Bastian closed his eyes, willing his head to stop pounding.

"Was going to go to my room and clean up, but the way everything was spinning, I wasn't sure if I'd want to move again. I know we're supposed to play tonight, but I don't think I can. I didn't want to cancel via text. I didn't want to cancel at all. I thought about maybe not telling you what happened and trying anyway, but I really don't feel so hot."

Despite the throbbing in his head, he heard the sharpness of Jarrod's inhale, even as a gentle hand cupped his cheek.

"Let's see what the damage is," Jarrod murmured, lightly stroking his thumb over the pulse point on the side of Bastian's neck. "We can talk later about what you were going to do. Right now, I'm just happy you chose differently."

Unable to formulate a response, Bastian sat still while Jarrod retrieved a first aid kit and drew back the blinds to let more light into the room. While he knew it was so Jarrod didn't miss any of the damage he'd done to himself, the brightness did nothing for his head.

"Easy, sweetheart, just keep your eyes closed and let me take care of everything," Jarrod urged. "I think we need this t-shirt off first."

"Mmm 'kay." Bastian raised his arms so Jarrod could ease the shirt off him, groaning a little when the scrapes on the back of his shoulder pulled.

"I hate to say it, but I think the tree won."

Despite the circumstances, Bastian couldn't agree more, and even found himself laughing a little as Jarrod started cleaning his wounds.

"You've got quite a knot back here. Are you dizzy at all?"

"A little."

"Did you throw up?"

"No, but my stomach was a little uneasy at first when everything was spinning."

Strong fingers rubbed the back of his neck with a tenderness that was bone melting. "I'd like to put some ointment on the scrapes, but a shower might be in order first. Do you think you can manage to lean against the wall and let me do all the work?"

"I can manage anything if it means I get to lay down soon."

"It does, but I'm also going to page the event's medic and have him come up and take a look at you."

"Isn't that what you're doing?"

"I can treat the cuts and scrapes, but that head injury is a different story. They're nothing to play around with. You could have a concussion, and if that's the case, then we need to know so we know what signs to look out for if it starts getting worse."

"Can't it wait until later?"

"No."

It was a firm refusal, spoken in a voice that clearly said don't argue, and all without raising the volume even a little. In no time at all, Jarrod had him beneath the shower spray as he rubbed soap over Bastian's body before carefully washing his hair.

"Next time we do this is going to be a lot more fun," Jarrod said as he worked. "Provided you don't go taking on any more trees."

"And benches, and hedges," Bastian grumbled as the water ran down his face.

"What?"

"It wasn't a good morning even before the tree. Chauncy and I got into an argument while I was changing into my workout clothes. Was like he was waiting on me to come in just so he could start something about me sleeping over here with you. I guess between thinking about him and thinking about you, I was hella distracted."

Jarrod's lips on the back of his neck were soft as they trailed kisses down his spine. "While I'm glad that you think of me when we aren't together, I'd like it much more if you could manage it without hurting yourself."

For the second time since he arrived, Bastian managed a laugh. Jarrod rinsed him off, towel dried him and wrapped him in a bathrobe before leading him back out into the main room. He'd no sooner gotten Bastian settled on the bed when a knock announced the arrival of the medic.

"So, I hear someone had a bit of an accident." He had a cheerful voice and long salt and pepper hair that he wore tied back from his face. He looked nothing like any medic Bastian had ever seen, which was plenty considering how many years he'd been practicing parkour. His uniform was leather and denim, from old school biker cap to highly polished boots. When Bastian met his gaze all he saw in that muddy hazel was compassion and concern.

"I'm Scott, though everyone just calls me Scoundrel. I suppose I come by it honestly enough. And who might you be?"

"Bastian."

"Nice to meet you, though I'm sure you'd have preferred it to be under better circumstances."

Bastian started to nod, only pain won out and he settled for a muttered, "Yeah."

"Well, let's see what you've done to yourself."

The whole time he was talking, he'd been pulling things out of his bag, while Jarrod had sat on the bed beside him, slid an arm around him and hugged him close.

"Oh yeah, you've got a nasty bump, lost a chunk of skin too, though it's not so deep that you need stitches," Scott said as he examined the back of Bastian's head. It was when he came around to stand in front of him and shone a bright light in his eyes that Bastian winced and tried to look away.

"None of that now, I'll be done in a moment," Scott assured him, keeping his tone light and low. "Was there ever a moment when you lost consciousness?"

"No."

"But you were dizzy?"

"Yeah."

"How about now?"

"No, it's faded. My head still hurts though."

"I bet it does. These old trees have been around for a long time, they've had plenty of opportunity to grow sturdier than the human skull. If you can take over the counter pain pills, go ahead and take them for however long you need to, just be careful not to go over the daily dose."

"He won't," Jarrod remarked in that steely voice of his.

A look passed between them, one Bastian wasn't sure what to make of, it was like they were communicating without words, then Scoundrel gave a curt nod and turned his attention back to Bastian.

"Any ringing in your ears?" Scoundrel asked.

"No."

Scoundrel waved a massive hand in front of his face, waiting for Bastian to focus on it before asking, "How many fingers am I holding up?"

"Three."

"Is he going to be staying here with you for a bit?" Scoundrel asked Jarrod.

"Yup."

"Good, just keep an eye on him and touch base with me if he starts displaying any of the signs on this pamphlet," Scoundrel said, passing Jarrod a red and white rectangular sheet of paper with a whole lot of words printed on it.

"Will do." Jarrod replied.

"Good, now, I've got a couple words I'd like you to remember," Scoundrel said, turning his attention back to Bastian, "Do you think you can do that?"

"I can try."

"Good enough. Rodent. Water. Gecko. Purple. Peace."

Bastian repeated them back to him, earning a nod.

"Good, now I'm going to call back up here a little later and see if you still remember those."

"Okay," Bastian replied, barely stifling a yawn.

"It's okay to let him sleep if he wants to," Scoundrel advised. "Just make sure you wake him every few hours, and touch base with him on how he's feeling. Any issues and you have my number."

"Thanks again for coming up," Jarrod said.

"No problem. Does he have a training session today?"

"Not until Monday," Bastian muttered.

"Okay, see how you're feeling then and make sure you let your trainer know what happened, so he can keep an eye on you. I don't think you have a concussion, you just got your bell rung real good, but we're not going to take any chances, okay, so take it easy and let Jarrod be good to you while you heal up."

"That's easy enough to do."

"Good."

When Jarrod started to get up the big man waved him off. "I can see myself out. You stay with your little one and see to it that he gets some rest."

Rest sounded real good, and the bed felt so comfortable beneath him that it was easy to curl on his side and sink into the bedding.

"Would you like something for your headache?" Jarrod asked.

"Yes, please."

Two pills were pressed into his hand, and when he raised his head, a bottle of juice was held to his lips. He swallowed enough of it to get the medicine down before he stretched out again. It wasn't so much that he was sleepy, he'd gotten plenty of rest the night before, but his head felt like an angry woodpecker was trying to escape, and that, in and of itself, was draining.

"One more thing to take care of before you rest," Jarrod said holding out Bastian's phone, with its bright purple dragon case.

"What am I supposed to do with this?" Bastian grumbled, accepting it and moving to shove it beneath his pillow.

"I know you two are fighting, but you really should let Chauncy know what happened," Jarrod advised. "Especially if you start to feel worse, and it becomes necessary to take a trip to the hospital. I'm willing to bet that you're each other's medical contacts while you're here."

"Yeah."

"Then get to texting."

Jarrod's words, spoken in a no-nonsense tone, soon had Bastian's fingers fumbling over the keypad. When he was through, he put the phone on silent before shoving it beneath the pillow, where he could feel it if it vibrated. Sure enough, he'd no sooner withdrawn his hand that he received a response from Chauncy filled with questions and a demand that Bastian returned to their room where he could look out for him.

He declined, but thanked Chauncy for his concern and promised he'd text and tell him how he was feeling once he'd had a nap.

Chauncy's follow up reply was a sad faced emoji accompanied by a threat to come hunt him down if he didn't hear from him before dinner so Bastian ended the discussion with a promise that he would. By then, his head was pounding worse and his vision had grown blurry. Closing his eyes helped the pounding a little, but he knew that nothing but rest would make it go away completely.

"Thanks for looking out for me," Bastian murmured when he felt the bed dip as Jarrod stretched out beside him.

"Did you really think I wouldn't?"

"Just wasn't sure if this was something to concern you with," Bastian admitted as he hugged the arm Jarrod draped over him. "Then I remembered what you said, 'bout how I should ask if I wanted to know something, so I did."

"And it's a good thing too, what if you'd been hurt worse than you were?"

"Yeah." Bastian conceded, having suffered through the effects of a concussion before, alone and curled in his blanket nest until his uncle had stopped in to check on him and found him dazed and disoriented. That had necessitated a trip to the hospital that he still didn't remember clearly, unlike the lecture his uncle had waited to give until he was feeling better.

"Listen to me carefully, little one, and listen good," Jarrod said, voice firm and stern despite how low he kept it. "Playtime can always be moved. I will never be upset or disappointed if you don't feel up to it, quite the opposite, actually. I'll be proud of you for being honest with me and not trying to force yourself to do something you aren't going to enjoy. I don't ever again want to hear that you thought of concealing an injury from me. If you're hurt, I want to know about it so I can take care of you because that is what my job is supposed to be. It's what we talked about, remember?"

Jarrod was right. Bastian knew he'd almost made a costly mistake, especially when it came to trust. "Uh-huh."

"Good. I'm glad you came to me and told me what happened. We'll reschedule playtime when you're feeling up to it, for now there is something I'm quite pleased about."

"What's that?"

"Having a whole day just to cuddle you."

Chapter 12
Whispers in the dark, an impromptu story hour

Two forty-three in the morning and Jarrod felt Bastian wiggle and shift against him for the seventh time in less than an hour. Knowing that his pet was struggling to sleep was making it difficult for Jarrod to succumb to slumber, despite the press of exhaustion weighing him down. He'd been waiting to see if Bastian would say anything, ask for another pain pill or Jarrod to rub the back of his neck and shoulders again, since he'd admitted earlier in the day that the muscles were sore and a bit stiff after yesterday's run in with the tree. So far his pet was proving stubborn though, not that Jarrod expected any less.

He understood Bastian's fierce independence and didn't want to do anything to curb that or make him feel smothered. Time was what they needed for Bastian to learn the difference between being needy for the sake of seeking attention and earnestly needing something. Of course, he also had to be willing to let Jarrod give it to him, though that hadn't seemed to be a problem so far. No, the issue was Bastian admitting he needed anything in the first place.

Just when he was about to announce to his pet that he was awake and aware that Bastian was too, his little one surprised him by rolling over and nuzzling against his chest.

"Jarrod?"

He'd kept his voice low but clearly hopeful. Jarrod knew what that meant. His little one would lie there occasionally squirming all night if he couldn't settle down to sleep.

"I'm awake sweetheart, what's bothering you? Is your head hurting again?"

"No," Bastian murmured, voice partially muffled against the blankets Jarrod was burrowed in. "I'm just having a hard time staying asleep. Would you talk to me a little?"

Awe. Jarrod hugged him close and kissed the top of his head. "Sure, what would you like to talk about?"

"I dunno, just, anything I guess."

Chuckling, Jarrod rubbed circles on his back. "Well, let's try and narrow it down a little, shall we?"

"Okay. How do we do that?"

"Well, let's see, when we were talking about movies the other day, you said you loved fantasy," Jarrod murmured, keeping his voice low and soothing in the hopes that it would help Bastian grow drowsy enough to get a bit more sleep.

"Do you have a favorite type of creature, besides hobbits and elves?"

"I like the dwarves too, but I love dragons. When I first started drawing, I filled pages in my sketchbooks with them, most of them horrible and completely out of proportion."

"Have you ever seen a dragon?"

"Just the ones in movies."

"Then how do you know you got the proportions wrong?"

Jarrod was coming to learn that when he said something unexpected, something that made Bastian stop and reconsider his own position, his little pet got quiet and contemplative. It was a good trait when one really took the time to think about it. It not only meant that Bastian listened, but it showed he was willing to consider things from different points of view.

"I guess I never considered it that way. I just kept practicing and practicing until I could make mine look like everyone else's."

"See, now that's a problem right there. Why be like everyone else when you can be you?"

"Yeah. I guess I didn't think anyone would like my versions if they were different."

"Is being liked that important to you?"

Again Bastian paused, while Jarrod cuddled him, curious to hear his answer.

"Doesn't everyone want to be liked?"

"It depends on what you're being liked for. Do you want to be liked for following the crowd and doing what everyone else does, or do you want to be liked for who you are and what you can bring to the world?"

"I–I guess I just wanted not to fuck up."

"Ahh, I see," Jarrod murmured, thinking back to the conversations they'd had about Bastian and school and how critical his family had been about his efforts, especially when he didn't bring home the same grades and accolades as some of his siblings did. "So, what did you intend to do with your dragons, once you got them to look the way you wanted?"

Bastian let out a short snort of laughter that even muffled had an edge of sarcasm to it. "Was gonna make a book, with illustrations and stuff, but I don't know, by the time I got done working out how to make the dragons look right it wasn't fun anymore. I wrote the story in the back of my math notebook though. It was about the only time it ever got used."

Jarrod chuckled at that. "You mean back in the days when paper actually got used in school."

"I know, right? By my senior year, they issued everyone computers. We didn't even have textbooks anymore, which was nice, 'cause they were heavy as hell and I tended to forget mine in my locker anyway. Was no way in hell I was carrying them around in my backpack all day, but it always seemed like my classes were clear across the school from where my locker was."

"I remember those days well," Jarrod said. "I was fortunate enough to have a friend with a locker on the other side of the building from mine, so we'd stash our stuff in each other's lockers to make it easier to get to the books we needed without being late for class. Was still a pain in the ass though. Eight notebooks, six textbooks, folders and pens and whatever else the teachers asked for. I imagine computers made things much easier."

"Meh," Bastian grumbled, sighing, and falling silent.

"What was the story about?" Jarrod asked, hoping to shift his thought away from his issues in school.

"It was stupid."

"Why don't you let me be the judge of that?"

Bastian squirmed against him, but Jarrod didn't let go, instead he played with Bastian's hair until he settled down again.

When Bastian finally spoke, his voice held a note of caution. "You really want to hear it?"

"Please."

"Okay, but…I was like, fifteen when I came up with it."

"So?"

Jarrod waited for Bastian to think up another protest, pleased when he huffed in that way of his that Jarrod had come to know meant he was done being difficult, at least for now.

"Don't say I didn't warn you," Bastian finally grumbled, humming a little. "This one morning, really early I was laying in the hammock by the campfire watching the smoke curl up toward the treetops and, I don't know, one of the swirls sorta looked like a dragon. In my head, I started thinking about this dragon that could control smoke and shadows. It could even slip into homes through the locks and the cracks where the windows didn't seal well."

"Talk about unique, I like it."

"I did to," Bastian admitted. "At first I was going to make him a thief, but I didn't want him to be bad, I wanted him to be looking for something more important than just some relic or jewel. I always felt like dragons got a bad rep in some folklore, that they were written as being greedy things that took and horded and guarded stuff fiercely. Lived alone in caves and lonely places beneath the ground, eating anyone who dared to stumble upon its lair."

"Yeah, that is kind of one sided, when you think about it. I don't remember many stories where the dragon was good, except maybe the one in *DragonHeart*," Jarrod said. "Oh and Puff, though I've always wondered about that song and whether it really was made for children."

"Same."

"So tell me more about your dragon?" Jarrod prodded when it seemed like Bastian was going to fall silent again.

"Well, he um, his name was Rowan, and he was looking for the other half of his soul," Bastian explained. "You see, a long time ago, when there was still magic in the world, the king of the warlocks and the queen of the dragons had a disagreement. Both insisted they were right. The warlock wanted to claim one of the queen's daughters as his mate, and the queen forbade it, because she foresaw nothing but ruin for both of them. She tried to explain her vision to the king, but he refused to listen, insisting that he could make the princess happy in his kingdom and that the queen was being cruel and heartless by keeping them apart. Though she tried to tell him all the ways that a marriage with the princess would be disastrous for the king he grew angrier and angrier. He tried to take the princess from her mountain home by force, but the queen protested. The king and queen battled and in the chaos, the warlock smashed the great silver orb that contained all the souls of the unborn dragons."

"Whoa…" Jarrod breathed, held spellbound by the story that Bastian was sharing with him. This was no cute, fluffy story to grace the shelves of a second-grade classroom; this had the makings of something dark, like an old piece of animation that had been his mother's favorite. Though in that one, it had been unicorns driven into the sea by a glowing bull because a king wished to keep them all imprisoned in the ocean. Damned if he could think of the name of the movie now, but he could picture that scene in his head, of the bull trying to force the unicorn into the sea.

"When the orb shattered the souls were blown away by the ferocious storm the warlock had conjured. Torn between protecting her child and rescuing the souls before they were lost for good, the queen chased after the souls, and the warlock took the princess and left the queen's realm."

"Something tells me this story doesn't have a happy ending."

"I guess it all depends on who you're rooting for," Bastian admitted.

"Fair enough."

"At first, all appeared well and the warlock took great pride in his new bride and constantly disparaged the queen's visions and bragged that he'd been right and she'd been wrong. Then little things started happening for which he couldn't explain."

Jarrod yawned, despite how drawn to the story he was. While he eagerly awaited the next sequence of events, it was a struggle to keep his eyes open, and he wondered if Bastian had any idea of what a wonderful storyteller he was.

"Are you sure I'm not boring you?"

Clearly, he didn't. Damn. Jarrod hugged him tighter and pressed a kiss to the top of his head.

"Not in the slightest, in fact, I'll be highly disappointed if I don't get to find out how this story ends," Jarrod admitted, stifling another yawn. The last thing he wanted was for Bastian to think he wasn't interested, though sleep, especially due to Bastian's wonderful tale, was certainly creeping up on him.

"Well, you know how I said that Rowan was a smoke and shadow dragon?" Bastian asked.

"Yup."

"The princess was a dragon of chaos, and her powers were bound, but only as long as she remained in her mother's keep. When the warlock took her from it, the spell broke.

Minor arguments in the king's stronghold turned into battles between witches and warlocks and it wasn't just the magical folk who were affected. Soon his subjects and even the creatures of his kingdom were fighting. They stopped tending to their homes, they stopped doing their work, they just stopped, and families quickly began to break apart. Some stayed in the kingdom, some left, and many things were damaged and destroyed."

"I'm surprised he let the princess stay, if she was causing so much hostility," Jarrod mused.

"He didn't know," Bastian murmured.

He was starting to sound sleepy now too, the occasional word slurred as he told the story. Bastian sighed and slid his arm beneath the blanket that was draped over Jarrod, wrapping it around him and making Jarrod shiver from the contact with that cold appendage. They'd come up with a way of sleeping that worked for them. The air remained on, the room at a temperature Jarrod typically preferred only in summer, but with the blankets, including the extra one Bastian had brought down from his room, Jarrod was toasty.

"The queen loved her child and wanted to protect her. She didn't want the princess to know how destructive her abilities were, not when so many around her could use their abilities to create. The queen knew that in a time of war, her daughter's abilities could be used against their enemies, but she'd worked hard to secure peace, and could never imagine using her child as a weapon. Instead, she allowed her child to believe that her powers came from her songs, which always had the ability to make others happy."

"Music has a way of doing that," Jarrod mused. "You take a single song and play it all over the world and no matter where they are, people can relate to the emotions even if the experiences aren't familiar to them."

"Yeah. That's kind of what I was thinking about when I was writing the story," Bastian admitted. "Only because we were learning about the anti-war movement and how some of those songs were used all around the world."

Hearing that, it amazed him that Bastian truly believed that he'd been a poor student and a failure in school. It sounded to Jarrod like his little pet had learned plenty, at least about the things that had truly interested him. In fact, the longer Jarrod listened to Bastian weave his tale, the more he learned about the depth and complexity of Bastian's soul.

"It was the princess who finally realized she was the reason the kingdom was falling into ruin," Bastian said, continuing his story. "She'd happened upon two blue jays happily singing in a tree, and because she loved music so much, she stopped to listen. The longer she stayed there the more the tone of the song changed, and soon, the jays were fighting, pecking and tearing at one another's feathers and dripping blood everywhere. She knew then what she had to do."

"I know it's just a story, but I hope the jays lived." Jarrod mused.

"They did, after the princess fled the clearing, and the kingdom," Bastian explained. "She returned to her mother and begged her help, which her mother was happy to give, binding her powers again, but the damage had been done, both to the warlock's kingdom and the dragons, since the queen had not been able to rescue all the souls."

"Which was why Rowan was looking for the other half of his," Jarrod said as pieces of the story came full circle and it dawned on him what a truly intricate story Bastian had woven, especially at such a young age.

"Uh-huh," Bastian said, sounding both pleased and tired. "And he found it too, in the being who was meant to be his mate."

There was an intimacy in this moment that Jarrod had never felt with anyone else. He'd always known that sex and intimacy were two completely different things, but never before had anyone proven it to him like this. Jarrod tried to imagine what it would be like to lay in bed together and talk about their day, and it hit him then that while he and Bastian would soon be separated by hundreds of miles, there were things they'd be able to do to make the distance feel less glaring.

Like getting tucked in their favorite positions in bed, a pillow to simulate where the other should be, phones pressed to their ears, or on the pillow beside their heads, speakerphone letting them communicate until one or both of them passed out. While it wouldn't be the same as having his pet in his arms, if he closed his eyes, he knew he'd be able to draw on this moment to carry him through.

"As long as the souls were in the orb, the queen could ensure that they were placed inside a baby dragon while it was still in its egg," Bastian explained. "But once they were scattered on the wind, they wound up in all sorts of creatures, making it much harder for dragons to find their mates and when they did, there was never a guarantee they could have any children, and so, as time went on, they began to die out."

"And the warlocks?"

"Decimated," Bastian explained, yawning. "They never did recover. Too much damage was done. Too many things had happened that couldn't be taken back. They became solitary wanderers, those that survived anyway."

"Was Rowan's mate a dragon too?" Jarrod asked, still curious about that aspect of the story.

Bastian sighed contently, a soft, sleepy sound. "Not exactly. His mate was born human, but with a dragon's soul, which meant that once Rowan found him, he could become a dragon too, and they could go on to have their happily ever after, ruling the smoke and shadows of Rowan's realm."

Jarrod took a moment to fully appreciate the ending and let it sink in. "That was pretty damned awesome. Thank you for sharing it with me."

"Really?"

"Yes. Really. I loved it," Jarrod admitted. "Not only that, but I don't think you should leave it languishing in an old notebook. I think you need to dust it off and do something with it. It's too fabulous to just sit on a page forgotten about."

"Mmmm maybe." Bastian yawned again and muttered something Jarrod couldn't make out, and for a moment, he thought maybe his pet was finally drifting off to sleep.

He kissed the top of his head and murmured a soft, "Pleasant dreams."

"Will you go for a walk with me in the morning?" Bastian grumbled, the words so soft and garbled that for a moment, Jarrod wasn't certain of exactly what it was he said.

"Doesn't have to be early. I really don't wanna get up early for once."

"Then we'll sleep in," Jarrod offered.

"M 'kay."

"And I can always go down to the restaurant and pick up breakfast for us," Jarrod said. "I can't promise it will be as nice as our picnic, but how do blueberry crepes sound to you?"

"Wonderful."

"Yeah."

"Fluffy good."

Jarrod chuckled and lightly stroked his hair.

"Do they have whipped cream as well as syrup?"

"I'll bet they do."

"Sounds so good. Sometimes I like to have breakfast for dinner."

"Really? That sounds like fun."

"My dad used to make pancakes when he had to make supper," Bastian said, his words getting harder to understand. "He'd put chocolate chips in them and make them look like a smiley face. They were so good. Mom used to get mad sometimes, 'cause that's all he ever made us, but they were the best pancakes in the whole wide world."

Bastian's breathing had evened out, and he finally seemed to be drifting off to sleep, while Jarrod lay holding him as the number on the clock changed from 4:33 to 4:34, thinking of how lucky he was to have looked out the window and seen a streak of red and gold flipping past, trying to defy gravity.

Chapter 13
What a difference a little care makes

"I have a present for you," Jarrod announced, sitting on the edge of the bed and carding his fingers through Bastian's hair. In the three days since his little accident, Jarrod had walked with him in the morning, so he didn't have to completely break his workout routine. He'd brought fruit and omelets oozing cheese and mushrooms, and just this afternoon he'd accompanied Bastian to his training session, watching from a corner of the room, after informing Daddy William of what had happened to him.

Rather than feeling smothered and overwhelmed, all Bastian felt was cozy and well-cared for. Well rested too, now that he'd moved into the room with him permanently. Chauncy had sent him a text that they needed to talk, and Bastian had assured him that they would, over dinner later that night. At least now that his headache was gone he felt like he could handle another confrontation with him, though he hoped it ended more amicably than last time. As much as he enjoyed Jarrod's attention, the shimmer of it was dulled by the knowledge that he and Chauncy's friendship was fractured.

The package Jarrod slipped into his hands was flat, like a greeting card, but there was a bit of weight to it too. A bright neon green ribbon secured the paper, and Bastian fumbled a bit to untie it before he got it loose. What he unveiled looked like a miniature checkerboard, only the heading at the top read Ferret Bingo.

"I thought we could play it together."

"Don't we need more people for bingo?" Bastian asked. "And numbers?"

"Not this kind of bingo."

"Why not?"

"It's just for you and me, and instead of numbers, we're going to be putting a sticky note over each square, once we come up with a goal to put on it."

"I don't get it."

When Jarrod cupped his face in his hands and locked eyes with him, Bastian felt the immediate urge to squirm and look away. The whole moment was too intense, but that earnest look in Jarrod's eyes stilled his movements and in the end, Bastian simply held still and listened.

"In the short time I've come to know you, you've mentioned several things other people felt you were deficient at," Jarrod said. "It dawned on me that you put too much stock in that, and not enough faith in yourself and what you're capable of, so, I started looking for ways to encourage you, and came across this."

"Okay…I guess."

"Hey, this is not me looking for a way to try and change you," Jarrod insisted. "I want you to come up with the goals you want to accomplish, all I'm asking is for you to let me help you get there."

Bastian nodded. He thought he got it, but he wasn't completely sure. "So, if I wanted to put 'add meditation to morning routine' on there, that would be a goal?"

"Exactly. We could even break it up in a way that would let you succeed multiple times."

"How do we do that?"

"Well, we could put something like 'meditate Monday morning' as one goal, then have another goal for Tuesday, and so on, that way you have daily successes. You could even set different amounts of time for each day, that way you can see what works well for you, and what you might have to work up to."

"Let's do that."

Bastian watched as Jarrod started writing things out on the sticky pad and putting each little square over one on the board. They fit perfectly, while still allowing the lines on either side of them to show.

"Would you consider it a goal to be able to sit through a movie I've always wanted to see but never had the patience to focus on?"

"I would indeed."

"Then let's put that down too," Bastian said. "And I really need to come up with something better than a day planner for organizing my day with. I never have it on hand when I need it, so I wind up scribbling things on little slips of paper, then losing the slips of paper and having to go back through my emails and texts to figure out what the hell I was supposed to do."

"Okay, that definitely sounds like something we can put on the sheet to work on."

Now that he had the hang of it, it was easy for Bastian to come up with a list of things he struggled to accomplish, and with Jarrod's help, break them down into goals he might actually be able to achieve. Of course, when he'd phrased it that way, Jarrod had devised another goal for him, one that involved him saying positive things about himself rather than putting himself down.

"Now we just need a rewards list and we'll be all set," Jarrod said, tapping his pen on the notepad he held.

"That's easy, any kind of fruit is fine with me."

When Jarrod tugged him closer, chuckled and kissed the side his head, Bastian found himself wondering what was so funny.

"I was thinking of something a little more…fun."

"Oh. Ohhhhh."

"Now you're getting it, though, I will certainly be keeping fruit around for your playtime treats," Jarrod said. "I know how much you enjoy it. Is there anything else you'd like me to add?"

Bastian could feel little furrows forming between his eyebrows as he thought about it, but every image that came to mind was a melon or berry. "Not really."

"No worries. If you think of something later I can always add it."

Nodding, Bastian felt his face heat up, because there were a few things that had come to mind now that he understood the type of rewards Jarrod had been referring to. "Can we play with wax?"

"Right now?" Jarrod asked, glancing at his bag in a way that left Bastian wondering if he already had everything he'd need in order to indulge him, or if he'd have to go out and get a few things before he could make that happen.

"As one of the rewards," Bastian said, though it was on the tip of his tongue to beg for it now. The only thing that held him back was the knowledge that Jarrod had scheduled an extra training session with two of his ponies, and it was set to take place in just a little while.

"That's exactly the kind of thing I was thinking of."

"Were you also thinking about soft ropes and nipple clamps?"

"I can be."

"Yes please."

Jarrod reached over, tweaked one of his nipples, then wrote that down too, smirking at him while he did it.

"Can one reward be getting to ride your cock?"

"Absolutely. You'll hear no arguments out of me about that."

As their list grew, so did Bastian's excitement, though a little something did nag at him.

"What if I fail in a goal?" he asked.

"You can't, the game isn't set up that way."

"Really?"

"Yup. You get as many attempts as you want, and if there ever comes a point when you want to replace a goal, you can do that too, no questions. I want this to be fun for you," Jarrod explained. "And I want it to be something we can do from a distance too. I've already made a second card so we can synch them up when we're apart."

"Sometimes it feels like you're too good to be true."

"Why?"

"Because no one does something like this for someone they barely know."

"They do if they want to get to know them better and become an important part of their lives. Let me ask you this, why are you looking for a loophole?"

"Because I'm used to them."

"Do you enjoy them?"

"No."

"Then don't you think it's time you stop having to put up with them?"

Sighing, Bastian nodded. Not only was Jarrod right, but all the things he'd been saying to him lately were things Bastian had already decided he was tired of.

"You do not have to accept behaviors you find unacceptable," Jarrod said. "Doing that not only disappoints you, but it lets the other party feel like it's something they can continue doing and get away with. We should never give positive reinforcement to negative behaviors."

"Yeah."

"I want you to remember that when you meet up with Chauncy tonight."

"I've kinda been dreading that."

"Why?"

"I just…I don't know if it's going to be a good talk, or another confrontation," Bastian admitted.

"What do you want it to be?"

"A conversation. One without name calling or accusations. I hate what I said to him and I hate that I let him push me into saying it."

"There you go," Jarrod said. "You need to make that clear to him, and if he won't listen, then you need to be prepared to put an end to the conversation before he pushes things that far again."

"The only way I can think to do that, without more words I can't take back, is to get up and walk away."

"And what's wrong with that?"

"Nothing, I guess, but…"

"No buts. You agreed to go sit down and have a conversation with him. You did not agree to subject yourself to more name calling and unreasonable demands."

"You're right. I know that. I guess I'm just worried about losing one of the only friends I've got."

"If he's truly your friend, he won't let himself be lost."
***

If he's truly your friend, he won't let himself be lost.

Those words had been resonating in Bastian's mind since Jarrod said them. He was still thinking about them when he stepped into the hotel restaurant to meet Chauncy for their talk. What he hadn't expected was for his friend to already be there waiting for him. A quick glance at his watch showed that he was almost ten minutes early, which was commonplace for him, while Chauncy always seemed to run on what Bastian had affectionately called CST: Chauncy Standard time. That he'd broken that tradition tonight made Bastian weary, but he plastered a smile on his face and continued his path across the room.

"Hey," Chauncy said when Bastian approached the table. Since he'd seen his friend last, Chauncy had developed some dark circles beneath his eyes, and looked as if he'd gotten very little sleep.

"Hey yourself," Bastian said as he sat down, giving Chauncy's shoulder the slightest nudge. "You're looking a bit wrecked, did you have fun Saturday?"

"I didn't go."

"Oh."

"Was no use trying to have fun after how much of an asshole I'd been," Chauncy admitted. "I'm sorry, you didn't deserve the shit I was giving you."

"No, I didn't, but I get where the frustration came from," Bastian admitted. "I'm sorry you're not enjoying your time here."

"I want to, I really do, and I…well, I've come to realize there are things I could be doing to make it better for myself."

"Good for you."

"It's not like I came up with it on my own," Chauncy admitted. "Jarrod had a talk with me when he came to get your things, and well, he made some good points."

"He didn't mention anything about it to me."

"No, I don't guess he would. He said you hadn't put him up to it, that he was only approaching me because you cared about me and he cared about you and he hated seeing you upset because we'd been fighting."

Bastian nodded, grateful for the arrival of the menu, because words weren't coming to him in light of what he'd been told. Between the gift he'd been given this morning, and this, he was already half in love with the man. No one had ever looked out for him so completely, and all without asking anything in return.

Well, that wasn't exactly true. Jarrod had asked for his honesty, his trust, and the opportunity to see how things played out between them. In the grand scheme of things, it was everything Bastian could possibly want.

"Thanks to him, I realized that I've been going about some things all wrong," Chauncy said. "I've been sitting in the background waiting for someone to happen along and notice me, only, I haven't done anything to step out of my shell enough to be seen. I guess part of why I was so upset about the brat in class was because he had the nerve to do something I didn't, even if he was going about things the wrong way."

"Did something change there too?"

"Uh-huh, and I think Jarrod had a hand in that too. I know he spoke to my Trainer, I saw them together with another man. I think he helps organize things. They were talking before a session. I don't know what was said, but Master Cain stopped letting the brat have his way and the rest of us are starting to get more attention from him than we were before."

"I'm glad," Bastian replied. "Does that mean you're no longer thinking about leaving?"

"I was an ass for that too, and for calling you an attention whore. Jarrod told me how you guys met, that you were just doing your thing and he decided he needed to get to know you better."

"Pretty much. I'm glad he did though, I've never known anyone like him."

Their conversation was briefly interrupted when the waitress came to take their orders. Chauncy going for the chili and corn bread, Bastian opting to keep things on the lighter side with a garden salad adorned with ranch dressing and fried chicken chunks.

"Wait, you asked if I had fun like you didn't know I hadn't gone, didn't you go?" Chauncy asked once the waitress had left their table.

"No, after my little free-running accident I got to spend the weekend in bed being cared for by my new Keeper," Bastian admitted, a tingle of pride surging through him at getting to say that out loud. He just hoped it wasn't going to kick off another issue with his friend.

"Seriously?" Chauncy said. "You're together, together?"

"Yup. I um, we've talked a little about adoption day, but he doesn't really want to wait to collar me, not when I'm signed up for the auction. He wants to make sure that anyone who bids for me knows that I'm already taken."

"That's…awesome, actually," Chauncy said, and damn, his friend actually sounded sincere and happy for him. "Just like you. I really have been a shitty friend, getting jealous over good things happening for you, especially after the way Claude acted. You deserve to have someone who genuinely cares about you and wants to see you happy."

"Thanks. He really is amazing. This morning he gave me a bingo card he made, he laminated it and everything. It's…he found the layout for it online. It's called ferret bingo and it's for people with ADD. He filled it with things I can actually accomplish and each time I do, I get a sticker. When I get a bingo, I get a reward. I can't wait to start testing it out. It's one of the coolest things anyone's ever done for me and I…shit, I'm sorry, I really should watch how much I ramble and rave about shit like that. It's no wonder you get pissed off and frustrated with me."

"No. There's no reason you should keep the good things that happen to you to yourself, that's bullshit and I feel like a complete bastard for making you feel that way."

"Maybe, but I don't want you to feel like I'm rubbing it in either."

"You're not. Honestly. You never were. It was just me feeling insecure. I got used to being a big deal in college, and once I went to work for my old man it sort of translated over to there too. I can't remember the last time I had to work to meet people. I got used to them already knowing who I was and gravitating toward me. I guess I forgot that the rest of the world doesn't work the same way. Honestly, this whole event has been a good reality check for me. I can't believe what a spoiled brat I was being."

Bastian couldn't help but grin, grateful that his friend was coming to his senses. "It wasn't your finest moment, that's for sure."

Snorting, Chauncy nodded. "No shit. And to think I had the nerve to call that other kitten a brat. I mean, he was, but it's not like I was behaving any better."

"It's over and done with now. Let's just put it behind us."

"I'd like that. Thanks for being a real friend."

"Always."

Chapter 14
Fireflies and fudge-striped s'mores

"Close your eyes," Jarrod demanded, refusing to row any further until Bastian complied.

"Doesn't that defeat the point of being out here on such a beautiful evening?"

"It's only for a little while."

Bastian's eyes narrowed into a scowl, even as he gave Jarrod the cutest pout. "But the fireflies will be coming out soon."

"I promise they'll be plenty of time to enjoy them."

Bastian's huff reminded Jarrod of a small child told that he had to finish his supper before he could have dessert.

"Fine."

Even with his hands covering his eyes, he was still pouting, lips quirking every now and again, like he was trying hard not to laugh when Jarrod splashed water his way when he caught him peeking between his fingers.

"No cheating."

When he was sure he had Bastian's full compliance, he finished rowing them to their destination, docking their canoe in front of the site he'd spent all afternoon preparing.

"Please, can I open them now?" Bastian asked, his tone taking on a hint of a whine as Jarrod secured the canoe.

Chuckling, Jarrod reached forward and gently booped the end of his nose where it peeked out from between his hands. "Nope, not just yet. You have to be patient."

Bastian groaned but otherwise said nothing as he continued to wait impatiently. What mattered to Jarrod was that he waited with his hands still pressed to his face, and trusted Jarrod to guide him to his feet and up onto the dock.

"There you go sweetheart, good job. Shift just a little to the left now," Jarrod encouraged, directing him. Once he had Bastian exactly where he wanted him, he slid his hand over his pet's and whispered in his ear, "You can open them now."

Pressed against Bastian's back, he could feel the excitement vibrating through him as Jarrod guided his hands to his sides.

"Ohhhh," Bastian gasped, stiffening in his embrace. He started bouncing the moment Jarrod let him go, then he whirled, throwing his arms around Jarrod's neck, laughing as he hugged him.

"Was it worth the wait?" Jarrod murmured, stroking his back as Bastian continued to cling to him.

"Oh my god, yeah," Bastian said, pulling away, but only enough so he could kiss him. They melted together, Jarrod's hands tangling in Bastian's hair as they practically devoured one another. When his foot clanged against a lantern, Jarrod decided that might be a good time for them to get off the dock before they landed in the none-too-warm water. He took Bastian by the hand, leading him down the lantern lit dock to the tree-lined campsite that sat a little way off shore.

Jarrod had strung battery-operated fairy-lights between the trees, the brightness of them illuminating the blanket covered deck chairs that sat beside the fire pit. A cooler filled with the drinks and snacks Jarrod had driven over earlier was positioned between the chairs, along with a duffle bag filled with all the supplies he'd brought. It made a decent enough barricade between that part of the campsite and the other surprise he had arranged for Bastian.

His Jeep was up at the parking spot, a short walk away, since rowing back to the lodge after dark would prove too dicey, even by lantern-light, and he doubted his little pet would be up for sitting at the bow of the boat alone after everything Jarrod had in store for him.

"What's all that?" Bastian asked, pointing to the blanket covered mounds that lay on the far side of the chairs.

"The other part of your surprise," Jarrod explained, quickly catching Bastian's hand when he tried to hurry in that direction. "Hang on a moment, sweetheart, you're not ready for that yet."

"Oh…okay," Bastian muttered, though he had a hard time tearing his eyes off the area, which was exactly why Jarrod had covered things up so well. That and he hadn't wanted any of the woodland creatures to decide to use them as their playground before Bastian had a chance to enjoy them.

Chuckling, Jarrod framed Bastian's face with his hands and kissed the end of his nose before he tipped his head back and kissed him thoroughly, enjoying the way Bastian licked into his mouth, moaning with abandon.

"All will be revealed if you just have a little bit of patience," Jarrod promised. "Can you do that for me?"

"Uh-huh."

"Good now, before we can get started we've got to…" Jarrod began.

"Build the fire," Bastian blurted, eyes darting over Jarrod's shoulder, no doubt searching for the kindling and wood.

"Nope, that comes later, it isn't safe to have a fire yet."

"Ohh, do we need to rake up the pine needles around the fire pit first?"

"Well, we will probably want to do that, yes," Jarrod said, unable to finish his statement as Bastian flew past him, dropping to his knees beside the stone ring that surrounded the fire pit to start clearing away anything that could accidently be set ablaze by an errant spark.

His enthusiasm was infectious. Though it hadn't been at the top of Jarrod's list of things to do, he found himself helping his pet clear a wide circumference around it, if only because it would leave him with one less thing to do later. The moment Bastian reached for the kindling though, Jarrod stopped him and hauled him back against his chest, holding him securely. A fire might be nice right now, but it wasn't safe for what Jarrod had planned, especially when this would be the first time he'd be formally playing with his pet. Evening was likely to bring cooler temperatures, but once Bastian started playing, Jarrod knew he'd be more than warm enough.

"Nope...still not time for that yet." Jarrod declared, kissing the pulse point beneath his ear.

Bastian relaxed in his arms and hummed softly, a sign Jarrod took to mean he was ready to start receiving instructions.

"There are a few things we need to do first," Jarrod said keeping his voice low and firm, even as he maneuvered Bastian to the space between the chairs, where his duffel bag sat. Opening it, Jarrod began to remove pieces of Bastian's gear from it. "You'll be needing these things first."

Bastian let out a barely audible gasp, even as he began nodding. "Yes, please."

"Of course first, we'll need to get you out of those clothes," Jarrod said, laying each piece of gear in one of the chairs before standing and moving around behind Bastian.

Slowly, taking care and time, Jarrod stripped the shirt off over Bastian's head, kissing up his spine and along the back of his neck as he did, feeling each shiver that racked Bastian's body. Bastian's moans and contented sighs were music to his ears. He trailed feather soft caresses over Bastian's ribs, making him giggle and squirm. Here in this secluded space he could take his time teasing, licking over the goosebumps the wind raised along Bastian's arms.

"I bet you go shirtless when the weather is warm," Jarrod murmured. "Letting all this skin get sun kissed and shimmering with sweat. I can almost imagine your abs flexing as you arch into a backflip. The muscles in your legs standing out as you leap."

His fingers trailed over the sides of Bastian's legs as he peeled the sweatpants off him, Jarrod taking the time to tickle behind Bastian's knees and nip the skin on the back of his thighs.

"You're magnificent," Jarrod murmured. "You've made me so happy by allowing me the honor of being your Keeper and by trusting me to take care of you."

Bastian squirmed at the tickling but lifted each foot to step out of the material, one hand on Jarrod's shoulder for balance as Jarrod removed his shoes and socks too.

"I've been thinking about this all day," Jarrod said as he stepped back for a moment to admire Bastian standing naked with tendrils of sunshine and twinkling fairy lights slashed across his skin. His little pet had been shifting from one foot to the other, but as he stood there listening to the birdsong and feeling the breeze blow along his skin, he began to settle down. The sun was hanging low in the sky, though it hadn't yet begun to streak it with crimson. The evening was beautiful, but not more so than his pet, who stood watching him with longing and curiosity.

"Such a good boy, being so patient right now" Jarrod said as he stepped over to the gear and picked up the brown furry boy shorts he'd been dying to see his pet in. "I know your curious as to why I've brought you gear and my toy bag, but you're doing such a good job by not asking."

Bastian's face lit up with a smile, even as his eyes tracked Jarrod's every move.

"Can I help you into these?" Jarrod asked, coming to stand in front of Bastian with them.

Bastian's voice, when he finally found his words and responded, came out breathy with a hint of need. "Please."

"Hold on to me then," Jarrod said kneeling and waiting for Bastian to place his hands on his shoulders. "I don't want you falling over."

Bastian complied wordlessly, stepping into the shorts Jarrod held for him. The only sounds that came from him were giggles when Jarrod danced his fingertips up the sides of his legs. He didn't even say anything when Jarrod left the shorts hanging low on his hips with his junk exposed. Instead, he watched wide eyed as Jarrod rubbed his face over the shorts before standing once more.

"Do you want me to touch you?" Jarrod asked. "Make you feel good before I show you the other treats I have in store for you?"

Bastian nodded, but this was one time when Jarrod couldn't allow a soundless response to stand.

"Can you use your words for me?" Jarrod asked, reaching to gently stroke his hand over Bastian's head, his pet's hair feeling soft and silky beneath his fingertips.

Bastian nodded again, before finally managing an answer. "Yes, please."

"That's my good boy," Jarrod said, leaning in so he could plant a kiss on Bastian's forehead. His pet sighed and closed his eyes, the sunlight shimmering off his hair creating an almost halo-like effect.

Slipping around behind him again, Jarrod ran his fingers up his back before settling them on Bastian's shoulders, gently massaging before working his way down his arms and sides. All the soft play they'd done in their room up in the lodge had given him the chance to learn exactly what it took to fully relax him.

By the time he skimmed his fingertips down Bastian's abs on the way to his cock, he was leaning back against Jarrod, eyes heavy lidded, breathing slow and steady. Jarrod coated his hand with slick from the small bottle of lube he'd tucked in his pocket, making sure it was enough to create a nice slip and slide.

"Do you like my hand on your cock?" Jarrod whispered in his ear as he slowly closed his fingers around it, keeping his touch soft and light.

He felt Bastian nod against his shoulder and stroked him gently.

"I'm gonna make you feel so good," Jarrod cooed, licking the shell of Bastian's ear. "Making you come is just one of many treats I have in store for you tonight. I can't wait to see your face when you see the rest of them."

Light streaks of pink wormed their way through the spaces between the branches as Jarrod whispered a stream of praise and filth in Bastian's ear until his pet was whimpering and whining against him, letting out soft gasps and even softer babbering sounds. He didn't beg, he didn't plead, he just let his head fall back as he lost himself in the sensations of what Jarrod was doing to him until finally he let out a loud, shuddering exhale as he came all over Jarrod's hand.

In the afterglow, Jarrod held him close, committing the moment to memory. Ragged breathing melded with rustling leaves and squirrel chatter, the soft lap of water against the shore, and the distant cawing of crows several trees over. Jarrod kissed the top of his head and murmured praise in his ears, wanting Bastian to know exactly how free and uninhibited he'd looked, squirming against Jarrod. The wet wipes he'd placed on the edge of the lawn chair made cleaning his hands easy, even as Bastian clung to him.

"What a rare and beautiful treat you've given me," Jarrod said, as Bastian's breathing finally began evening out. "To see you coming like that with the sunlight slashed across your face and the wind ruffling your hair. Makes me feel like we're the only two people in the world."

Bastian hummed, a soft contented sound as he turned enough to nuzzle the side of Jarrod's neck. Jarrod stroked his hair and back, allowing him to remain that way as long as he needed to. He'd could feel how loose and relaxed Bastian's muscles were, and the humming was a sure sign that he was inching closer to his ferret space. When Bastian tilted his head back and slowly opened his eyes, Jarrod could see the sunlight glittering in them, along with a peaceful sort of calm.

"Are you ready for your next treat?" Jarrod asked.

When his eyes widened a fraction, Jarrod could read the surprise in them, like he hadn't truly believed that there was more to come. Slowly he nodded, clinging to Jarrod a little before finally loosening his hold. Returning to the deck chair, Jarrod retrieved two more pieces of Bastian's costume.

"Do you remember when you said you wanted an obstacle course to play in," Jarrod asked, holding up two furry paws. Kneeling in front of his pet, he held one up so he could slide it onto Bastian's foot.

"Mmmm," Bastian replied as he lifted it so Jarrod could put the paw in place.

"I'd intended to make you one in the playroom the night we were set to go down," Jarrod admitted as he placed the other paw. "But then you had your little accident. I hated that you missed out on an evening of fun, but now that you're feeling better there's no reason we can't make up for it, just the two of us."

This time, Bastian responded with something that sounded an awful lot like another babber, the noise soft, but sharp, like his pet was excited. That was good. It meant he was slipping further into his pet space. As Jarrod slid the paws over his hands, Bastian bobbed his head a couple times and peered over Jarrod's shoulder, his attention finally brought back to the big surprise Jarrod had prepared for him.

His tail came next, attached to the shorts, rather than the one with the plug Bastian had admitted to only trying out on his own. That was something they could explore later, in a different sort of environment, once he'd gotten a feel for how his pet played. Jarrod peppered his face with kisses when he put the hood with the ears on him, making sure to take the time to draw out the moment, and stroke the ears once they were in place.

"There you are my adorable little ferret," Jarrod said as he adjusted the hood, making sure it was perfectly situated. "Come see what I've made for you."

Jarrod led him to the edge of the first blanket and pressed his palm to the side of Bastian's face. "Stay right here sweetheart, okay?"

Another head bob and babbering sound as Bastian offered assurance that he'd do as he was told. Leaving him there, Jarrod went and uncovered the obstacle course he'd created for Bastian to play in. With the help and permission of Daddy William, he'd brought several items from the playroom out here, including a huge flexible tunnel, a large plastic tube, several different sized balls, some large traffic cones, and a bright red tire that Daddy William had told him Bastian loved to climb through and be rolled around in.

Bastian's hands twitched and his smile grew about as wide as his eyes as he took it all in, but to his credit, even with his excitement showing, he stayed exactly where Jarrod had left him.

"Come here sweetheart," Jarrod said, eager to see his pet at play.

Bastian hurried to his side, but he didn't reach out to touch a single thing besides the hand Jarrod held out to him.

That he clung to and brought up to the side of his face, running his cheek against it.

"This is for you," Jarrod said, kissing his forehead before stepping out of his way. "You go enjoy it."

That seemed to be the only encouragement Bastian needed. He babbered and leapt over the tire, crawled through the tunnel, and sprawled on top of the tube, rocking it back and forth with his body before he took off again. The cones he slunk through, bobbing and weaving, before he returned to the tube again, crawling in it this time and making it roll. Jarrod got between it and the tree it was about to crash into, stopping it and sending it rolling the other way.

This was the reason he hadn't wanted the fire going just yet. Even pleasuring his pet and expending some of his energy hadn't dulled his enthusiasm too much. Bastian scampered and summersaulted, he draped himself over things, curled in them, and allowed Jarrod to roll him around in the tire, including weaving it between the cones.

Jarrod was pleased to see that despite the trees surrounding them being awful tempting on the trail runs Bastian took, he didn't make use of them tonight. Maybe it was the fairy lights that deterred him, or maybe he just truly enjoyed all the play items Jarrod had brought for him. Either way, it was one less worry, as Jarrod cautiously kept an eye on Bastian to keep him safe.

The blankets he'd laid out beneath the playthings kept Bastian from getting scraped up and dirty, and it was a good thing too, when Bastian wrapped himself around one of the balls, kicked at it with his feet, then rolled on his back so he could toss it in the air with them, batting it with his hands when it came back down.

It bounced off and Jarrod retrieved it, bringing it back and tossing it to him. He didn't so much catch it as bat it off his hands like a volleyball and soon the pair were batting it back and forth, Bastian babbering happily, the sound one that sent a surge of warmth through Jarrod's soul.

Their eyes met and Bastian crawled his way, Jarrod holding still to see what he would do. Bastian curled around his legs, head resting in his lap, letting Jarrod stroke his hair and lightly caress his neck and shoulders.

"I think playtime is over," Jarrod murmured, waiting to see if Bastian popped back up and scurried back to his playthings, but he barely twitched. His head was growing a bit heavy, suggesting to Jarrod that he was finally growing tired, a good thing too, since the sun was mostly gone now, taking much of the heat with it. "Come on, up you go."

The sound that came from him was a grumbled sort of babber, but he sat up and rubbed his head against Jarrod's cheek, making him laugh and hug his pet to him. "You can do plenty more of that once we get settled," Jarrod encouraged, helping Bastian up.

He guided him to the nearest chair and watched him curl on his side in it before Jarrod covered him up with blankets. While he had no intention of his pet remaining in his chair alone, he did have a fire to start and provisions to lay out so he could care for him. The kindling caught easily, soon growing enough that he could add the first chunk of wood. It was dry enough that it began crackling the moment the flames licked around it, and soon, a small measure of heat began emanating from it.

Each time he glanced over, he saw his pet tracking him with his eyes, the blanket pulled up around his face. A slight breeze ruffled the ears of his costume, making them dance a little. It was one of the most adorable sights Jarrod had ever seen. He made quick work of setting up the treats he brought, then scooped Bastian from his chair, blanket and all, to settle him on his lap in the other chair.

"Are you thirsty?" Jarrod asked, holding a leak proof water bottle to Bastian's lips so he could lap at the ball at the end of the tube. Bastian had expressed interest in trying out one of those small animal bottles to see if he could easily drink from in this headspace without accidently spilling all over himself, so Jarrod had picked one up. Now, as he watched his pet easily consume the juice Bastian had filled it with, he was glad he did. It worked perfectly for him.

When Bastian was done, he lay his head against Jarrod's shoulder and babbered softly, almost like a little song. It wasn't easy, but he was able to toast a few marshmallows, turning them into s'mores for him and gently feeding his pet from his hand. The fire was fully crackling now, and the mood was as peaceful and calm as anything Jarrod had ever experienced before. Sitting there with his pet in his arms, all he could think about was making this last well beyond the end of the event, maybe even forever.

Chapter 15
The moment of truth: Adoption Day

Bastian wasn't sure who was trembling more, him or Chauncy. They were backstage at the final day of *Pet Play by the Lake*, and it was soon to be time for adoptions. While Chauncy had wavered back and forth over taking part, he'd finally come to the conclusion that he wanted to see what it would be like.

I can't keep being scared to try new things. I need to put myself out there, even if in the end no one wants me.

Bastian hoped that wouldn't be the case. Despite the issues he and his best friend had struggled with at the start of the event, he knew Chauncy would make an amazing pet for someone. Bastian had already seen his confidence slowly begin to grow over the course of the training sessions, as he'd come to explore his kitten headspace and gain confidence as he played. It had turned out that much of Chauncy's hesitation had come not just from his natural shyness, but from how he viewed his body, especially when he was in his kitten suit.

When Chauncy ran his hands over the front of his fur for what had to be the eighth time in the last ten minutes, Bastian captured them and gave them a squeeze.

"What are you doing?" he asked, shocked when Chauncy dropped his gaze to the floor.

"Wishing I could make my stomach look a little smaller," Chauncy whispered. "I wish I'd gotten a larger size, then maybe I could hide some of my chunkiness in baggy fabric."

"There is absolutely no reason for you to do that," Bastian assured him. "You look adorable. I can't believe how awesome our makeup looks, thanks to you."

"I wanted to look as realistic as possible," Chauncy replied, squirming a little. It had taken coming here for him to learn to see that bit of body language for what it was, Chauncy being hesitant to accept even a little bit of praise.

"Well we do," Bastian said. "Just answer me one thing."

"What?"

"How many times did you have to watch *Cats* and practice in order to learn how to do this?"

"Not as many as you might think," Chauncy said. "Though I did watch the old and the new version back-to-back a couple times, just because I love them. I found tutorials online for the cat makeup, then studied ferret pictures and practiced until I'd come up with just the right variant of the makeup for you. Figured it was the least I could do...considering."

"Hey, none of that, we are never going to mention our little blowup again, got it."

"Yeah."

"I appreciate all that you did to create my look though, truly, just sitting there letting you put it on me helped settle my thoughts down some. I really needed that today."

If Chauncy's pawing at his suit had been repetitive, than Bastian didn't know what to call his own obsessive tendency to turn his attention to the doorway in the hopes of seeing Jarrod. Because of all the things they'd needed to do to get ready for the day, or in Jarrod's case, help his ponies get ready, they'd rolled out of bed and gone their separate ways.

For Bastian, that had meant hitting the trail and hurling himself through his free running routine, bouncing off so many things he'd wound up making himself dizzy after a series of corkscrew summersaults. He'd taken it a little easier after that, at least until he'd gotten to the hedges, then, with his usual breakneck intensity, he'd dived and rolled over them and even ended the run with several backflips and a handstand that had left all the blood rushing to his head.

He'd taken a long shower afterward too, only it hadn't had the typical effect of adding to his calm. Instead, he'd slumped against the wall with the water washing over him, stomach clenching and beginning to roil with anxiety.

The event was almost over.

Today was adoption day.

They'd talked about a collar or an ankle cuff, something to let the world know that he was Jarrod's, only he was going to be getting ready for it without either to put on. He'd tried not to think about it while Chauncy had been putting on his makeup, and done his best to hold still, not wanting to fidget and wreck his best friend's hard work.

It had been difficult though. His thoughts had been bouncing everywhere; from what he'd felt when he'd first arrived to what he was feeling as Chauncy was applying eyeliner with a thin tipped pen.

So much had changed.

He'd learned the difference between a Daddy, a Master, and a Keeper, as well as how someone could be all of those things and none. He'd learned that he didn't have to play as hard as he thought he did, that part of his struggle with reaching his pet headspace had been wrapped up in the issues with Claude. He'd learned that he was willing to welcome cuddles at any time, when they came from the right person, and that a good Keeper knew how to keep him safe without making him feel like he was being stifled.

He'd also learned what it felt like to fall in love, and that was what he was truly wrestling with at the moment. He'd wanted to say it last night. Hell he'd wanted to say it the morning after he and Jarrod's magical evening in the woods, only he'd refrained from doing it, afraid that Jarrod didn't feel the same way, and a strained, empty silence would descend between them if he allowed those words to spill from his mouth.

Now he longed desperately for his presence there, to have Jarrod touch base with him, maybe help him sink into the right headspace for when it was time to go out on stage. Only there was still no sign of him, and now Bastian was beginning to worry that maybe Jarrod had changed his mind about marking him as his before the bidding took place.

It was a charity adoption and Bastian knew all the money raised went to a very good cause. He also knew that the Masters who adopted pets on adoption day did so with the intent of taking them out and getting to know them. He didn't mind that part, not really, it was the uncertainty that left him feeling a little bit scared.

He'd meant to ask if Trainers ever bid on anyone, though what he'd really wanted to know was if Jarrod had any intention of bidding on him. The intrusive little voice in the back of his head pointed out the likeliness of Jarrod, as the Pony Master, preferring to bid on a pony. While Bastian was digesting that unnecessary smack to his already fragile sense of self, it raised its ugly head to point out another thing Bastian didn't need to think about. What if cutting him loose without a collar or cuff was Jarrod's way of cutting him loose period, without the tears and clinging of a messy goodbye.

Bastian liked to think he'd do a better job of that when the time came. That he'd be adult and dignified about the whole thing, not that goodbyes were ever easy, but he hoped he'd have tried his best to not make it harder on either of them, despite how attached he'd grown. Maybe Jarrod had sensed something in him that suggested differently and had sought to find them a simpler solution.

"Bas?"

Chauncy's voice cut through the haze of random thoughts pummeling him into a frozen state of panic and uncertainty. Blinking, he sought his friend's gaze and focused on them in an effort to pull out of the downward spiral he was working himself into.

"Sorry, what was that?" Bastian murmured, automatically assuming he'd missed something Chauncy was trying to say to him.

"Your hands are shaking," Chauncy said, stepping closer until he was pressed against Bastian's side. "You're picking at the seam of your suit and your breathing got all raspy. I've never seen you like this. What's wrong?"

"I just—" Bastian choked on the words, realizing in that instant that he was very close to tears.

"Come on Bas, talk to me."

"Jarrod didn't collar me like we talked about," Bastian whispered. "Or even put an ankle cuff on me. We'd talked about him clipping a little leash to the cage too, just so there would be something to let others know that even though I was taking part in the auction, I already belonged to someone, only now it feels like he changed his mind."

"Do you want to back out of the auction?"

"No, they've got everything all set up, and besides, I signed up because it was for charity. I thought that, with all the activities we were going to take part in, that if I met someone and they were interested in me, they'd be the one to bid on me. Only, I didn't take part in the pupnic and the other stuff 'cause I was spending all my time with Jarrod, so maybe now no one will bid on me at all." Bastian rambled.

"Do you want them to?" Chauncy asked, keeping his voice low. "You're starting to sound a bit confused."

"Because I am confused!" Bastian insisted.

"Take a deep breath."

"Huh?"

"Breathe in and hold it, the way we were taught. Count to three and then slowly let it out."

Bastian did as Chauncy told him, then did it again because the first time didn't do a damn thing for him. He felt Chauncy take his hand and lead him away from the milling bodies to a quieter spot near the shadows at the back of the space.

When Bastian opened his mouth to say something, Chauncy held up a finger, stopping it less than an inch from Bastian's lips.

"Shhh and just breathe and listen," Chauncy coached. "You're getting yourself all spun out. I'm sure Jarrod is around here somewhere. Maybe he's just tied up with one of his ponies."

There could be some truth to that. Bastian knew how much Jarrod cared about the ponies he'd been training and how important it was for him to make sure they all were comfortable with every aspect of the event.

Blowing out a breath, Bastian leaned into Chauncy's side, trying to convey to his friend how much he appreciated his help.

"We're going to be okay, no matter what happens," Chauncy told him. "As long as we've got each other, we'll at least have someone to laugh with later, when all of this is over. Cry too, if needed, but I hope that won't be the case."

Nodding, Bastian knew deep down that Chauncy was right. When they'd plotted out the route home they'd made certain it would be filled with interesting attractions, including the Oregon film museum, and sites featured in the film *The Goonies.* Bastian thought about all the images they'd viewed of Crater Lake National Park, and how much he looked forward to seeing the beauty of the wilderness there. While it would be a little like sticking a Band-Aid on a broken heart, he knew he'd be able to lose himself in the trip and not think too hard about the man he'd be leaving behind.

Only…

Breathe in. Breathe out, he reminded himself. He was not going to run through another list of onlys and what ifs. Instead, he closed his eyes and remembered the feel of Jarrod's hands in his hair, his lips on the back of his neck, his whispered words praising Bastian for waiting patiently, and being a good pet while Jarrod had been dressing him.

Two nights ago, Jarrod had helped him dress in his full fur suit and stretched him out on the bed in their room, music on low, and only a lamp to see by. He'd gone out somewhere, maybe the same place he'd found the small animal water bottle Bastian loved, and gotten a soft bristled brush, which he'd proceeded to spend a good hour grooming Bastian with. Through the suit, Bastian had been able to feel every stroke. It had caressed his body in such a gentle, rhythmic way, that Bastian had been lulled into pet space just by the feel of it. Nothing like that had ever happened to him before.

Jarrod had been so unhurried, and he'd talked to him the whole time too, telling Bastian about the time he and two of his friends had snuck into this old building that was rumored to be haunted, determined to film their own version of a paranormal adventure, complete with spending the night.

Between the ghost stories we told, and the creepy shit that kept happening, we just about scared each other to death. Turned out all the clawing and scratching was a family of raccoons who were a bit annoyed about us invading the place, but man did we abandon our plans of sleeping in different rooms.

Someone made announcement that it was time for all the pets to go their places, and Bastian's eyes shot open, a warm sense of contentment settling over him. Everything was a little soft around the edges, and he was so glad he and Chauncy were set up side by side, since that meant they could walk to their spaces together, holding hands the whole way. They hugged before they stepped into their respective areas, Bastian perching on the pet bed provided for him. There were toys there too, including a small rubber purple ball that he promptly balanced on his nose. It made Chauncy smile and sit up with his paws over the edge of the divider to watch him more closely.

Their spaces were big enough that Bastian could roll over on his back, squirm and make his tail swish. He'd worn the plug today, slipping it through the hole in the back of his suit specifically designed for it. Someone approached the front of his enclosure and dangled their fingers over the front, encouraging Bastian to rub against them. He was given ear rubs and light scritches as his reward, and a belly rub when he rolled back over again.

"Well now, aren't you just adorable," the man murmured, and Bastian preened and rolled so he could show off his trick with the ball.

He rolled around batting at the balls, wiggled and slunk and even slid his paw through the opening between his enclosure and Chauncy's to steal a ball. Chauncy mewed at him and swatted playfully, so Bastian batted it back through the hole, starting a whole other game. Someone dangled feathers on a string, first for Chauncy, then for him, encouraging them to play together as best they could with the barrier between them.

Time faded, sound dulled, until there was nothing but the games and praise. The faces changed, but the intent didn't. Daddy William appeared among the throng of those who visited with him, but unlike so many others, he lingered, stroking Bastian's fur and getting him to show off several of his tricks. Scoundrel visited too, paying special attention to Chauncy, calling him beautiful and encouraging him to play with several dangly things.

Someone moved slowly down the row. Bastian saw him putting labels on the placards in front of every cage, smiling at the pet inside before moving on to the next one. Bastian was proud to earn a smile as well and Chauncy got one too and more ear rubs from Scoundrel, who hadn't left his side.

Bastian sprawled across his bed, head pressed to Daddy William's thigh when his Trainer sat on the edge of his compartment.

"You did a good job, little one," Daddy William praised, drawing a soft babber from Bastian. "It sounds like you're getting tired though, did you have to wear yourself out before coming here today."

Bobbing his head, Bastian sought to convey to him that he had and was thirsty and hungry now, only Daddy William was no longer looking at him. He was checking his phone, scowling a little before a slow smile crept across his face.

In the enclosure next door, Scoundrel was gently wrapping an aqua ribbon around Chauncy's neck, tying it with a neat bow while Chauncy preened and softly mewed.

"I think he's ready for a snack, don't you?" Scoundrel suggested, looking Bastian's way.

"I'd say so," Daddy William replied.

Strong arms wrapped around him, gathering him into an embrace. Bastian curled against Daddy William's side, somewhere between pet space and the tranquil aftermath where everything was hazy anyway. There was certainly no bounce left in his step as they left the room. Seeing the playroom without any toys was a bit of a shock, but there was a blanket spread out in the middle of the floor with a variety of containers on it, just like the picnic beside the hedges that Jarrod had surprised him with.

His shoulders slumped and he pressed a bit tighter to Daddy William's side as he realized the auction had come and gone and Jarrod had never shown up, not even to check on him. Despite his suit he felt cold, and too tired for food though he'd eat to make Daddy William happy, because at least he hadn't abandoned him now that training was done.

He vaguely registered the sound of footsteps hurrying their way, then firm hands framed his face, tilting it so he could peer into the intense blue eyes staring at him.

"Sweetheart, I am so, so sorry," Jarrod said, kissing first his nose, then his lips, then all over his face until it looked like he was wearing lipstick from all the makeup Bastian had on.

For a moment, Bastian couldn't grasp what was happening. Daddy William was carefully easing away from him, while Jarrod kept gazing deep into his eyes.

"One of the ponies had a family emergency and completely broke down," Jarrod exclaimed. "There was no way I could leave him, sweetheart. He was one of my boys, my responsibility. I had to make sure all the arrangements were made to get him back home safely, especially with the mindset he was in. I sent you a text, only it dawned on me that you wouldn't get it because you'd be in your suit, so I sent one to Daddy William, so he could look out for you. I only just got back from the airport. I grabbed this on the way so I'd at least have something for you."

Jarrod was rambling the way Bastian's thoughts had been earlier in the day and with the way he was floating, Bastian wasn't sure he was grasping everything.

"Unfortunately, I didn't get to him before the event could start, got hung up with a little issue of my own," Daddy William explained. "He did a good job of getting himself where he needed to be and getting in the right mindset. You might want to slow down though, he doesn't seem to be tracking you."

Jarrod nodded and sucked in a breath, exhaling slowly. "Thank you. Do you know if he was adopted?"

"He was."

Jarrod's shoulders slumped and he let out a pained sigh. "Is there any way you can let them know that I'll bring Bastian to them once I've had the chance to care for him a little. I just, I need at least a half hour, an hour if you can convince them to wait that long. I don't want to make trouble for Lee and Shane over the auction, I just—"

"Relax kid, you already did."

Bastian watched as his Keeper blinked, a confused look crossing Jarrod's face, followed by one of stunned gratitude.

"I don't know how to thank you."

"Just be good to our boy here," Daddy William said. "He's a special little pet, he deserves to know that, don't you think?"

"Hell yeah."

"Then make sure to show him that so he never worries about not being enough again," Daddy William said before gently ruffling Bastian's hair. Turning, Bastian hugged the older Trainer who'd done so much to show him his potential.

"You keep on being the good boy I know you are," Daddy William said before kissing the top of his head. Bastian babbered softly in response, 'cause he'd do his best, he really would.

"Have a good time you two," Daddy William said before he turned to go, leaving Bastian to stare into Jarrod's eyes again.

"How about we sit and get you taken care of," Jarrod offered, holding out a hand, which Bastian was quick to accept.

Jarrod cupped his paw between his hands and gently led Bastian over to the blanket, where containers from a local seafood restaurant sat closed and waiting for them, the emblem on the top a dead giveaway of where Jarrod had stopped before his return. They'd talked about having dinner there before it was time to leave, and when Jarrod opened them to reveal what was inside, Bastian realized they were filled with all his favorite things.

His throat grew tight and he squeaked out a sound that was half babber and half sob. Jarrod gathered him in his arms before the tears could start falling, and held him while Bastian struggled to explain the turmoil of emotions he'd experienced earlier in the day.

"I though you'd decided you didn't want me after all," Bastian choked out as Jarrod rubbed circles on his back.

"Now where in the world did that come from?"

"The…you didn't…we talked about…" Bastian stammered, trying to think back through everything, included the wayward thoughts that had left him feeling so insecure.

"Awe sweetheart, if you only knew how badly I was kicking myself for not giving it to you this morning," Jarrod said. "But I'd wanted to make it special and put it on you where everyone in the room could see. I guess I was feeling a bit cocky. I didn't mean for you to ever feel like I wasn't going to keep my word."

It was a relief to hear that, and to know that the end of the event didn't have to mean the end of him and Jarrod. Bastian found himself swept into another hug, and felt kisses pressed to the side of his head.

"I've got it right here, see?" Jarrod said, gently shaking something until Bastian turned to look at it.

There was a black and purple box held in his hands, and when Jarrod opened it, he revealed the purple and silver bike chain collar nestled in its depths. Purple leather was woven between the links, and beside it sat a large metal charm in the shape of a ferret.

"I was lucky enough to find someone who did metalwork since ferrets are next to impossible to find," Jarrod explained. "She does amazing work, doesn't she?"

"Whoa…" Bastian murmured, completely blown away, especially when Jarrod turned the charm over to show the inscription on the other side. It read: *Lovingly Tended by Keeper Jarrod*

He hadn't used owned. He hadn't used property. Bastian's heart swelled with joy at seeing that. This was, in his opinion, a far more personal message.

"May I please put it on you?" Jarrod asked, holding the collar up.

Tears flooded Bastian's eyes as he nodded yes.

It wasn't too tight, it wasn't too heavy, and when Jarrod secured the charm to it with a little padlock, Bastian felt certain he'd found his person at last.

Chapter 16
Not the end, just a new beginning

"Please!" Bastian whined, wiggling his naked ass in Jarrod's direction. His riding crop lay on the bed, leather pressed to the side of his knee where he'd have easy access to it. It was the sting of it his pet was begging for, something they'd come to learn that Bastian dearly loved.

"I don't want you to be uncomfortable," Jarrod told him. "You've got a long ride ahead of you."

"But I want to feel it all the way home," Bastian pleaded. "I want to remember what you did to me and what you'll do when we see each other again."

"Well now, I wouldn't be a very good Keeper if I disappointed you now would I?"

"No."

"I do have one question first."

The sound Bastian made, part plea, part exasperated moan, made Jarrod's cock bob as he ached to bury it in his pet again.

"Now, now, we've talked about being patient, haven't we?" Jarrod cautioned in a rather teasing tone.

"Yes…sir."

"So, are you ready for my question?"

"Okay." He could practically hear the poutiness in Bastian's tone, but for the moment, he chose to let it go. If they'd had more time, he surely would have teased him longer, as it was they had…

Jarrod turned his head to see the clock glaring red numbers at him, informing him that they had less than two hours before they needed to check out. Not near enough time to do all the things he longed to do to his pet.

"My question is simple," Jarrod said, gliding his hand over the globe of Bastian's ass and lightly pinching one of the welts he'd already left there. "Do you want to feel me here…or here?"

With those last words he circled his finger around Bastian's hole, already puffy and slick with lube, open and more than ready for him.

"Oh my god, both, please, both," Bastian whined.

Well, if that was what he truly wanted, who was Jarrod to deny his pet. He pressed into him slowly, making sure he felt every inch of Jarrod's girth stretching him. Bastian shuddered beneath him, widened his knees a little more and groaned, though Jarrod was pleased to see that he didn't press backward and try and rush things like he'd done last night. His little pet was learning and that deserved a reward. Leaning over him, Jarrod kissed his way down Bastian's spine before firmly taking hold of his hips and shoving the rest of the way inside him, hard and deep, drawing groans from both of them.

He set a harsh pace too, nailing Bastian's sweet spot until he was trembling and crying out, then, with a devilish chuckle, he pulled out until only the tip lingered inside the rim of Bastian's hole.

His pet practically squealed in frustration, panting and whining and even letting out a babber or two, trying to urge him on again.

"Remember, this is what you asked for," Jarrod reminded him before pulling out completely. That greedy little hole winked at him, and Jarrod pinched the puffy rim just enough to make Bastian squirm, then he scooted back a little and took up his crop, delivering two stinging smacks, one to each ass cheek, before landing a perfect strike dead center, right on Bastian's hole.

His pet yelped at that, tensing a little and shivering. Jarrod rubbed circles over the base of his spine until he relaxed a little. "Too much?" he asked as he leaned in to kiss one of the welts.

"N–nooo."

"Are you sure?"

"Y–yes."

"Color?"

"Green, green, green!"

That was definitely a go in Jarrod's book. He repeated those strikes, wielding the crop with precision, only this time he dropped it after the final one and plunged back inside Bastian again, fucking him to the edge of orgasm before once again pulling back.

This time his pet whined curses and earned the stinging slaps with the crop that Jarrod delivered. His hole was puffy and red now and would certainly need a little bit of cream when they were through but Bastian cried out green when Jarrod checked with him again, and this time Jarrod fucked him until his pet came all over the sheets. Only then did Jarrod allow himself to come too.

By then moving was next to impossible for both of them. They curled together, Jarrod murmuring soft words of praise in Bastian's ear as his pet drifted in and out of consciousness. It was a good thing they'd packed almost everything the night before. If they made it to the desk to check out on time, it was going to be a minor miracle.

It was that thought, and the aftercare he knew his pet needed, that got him moving. It was slow going, coaxing Bastian to finish the water bottle Jarrod filled with the green sports drink Bastian had declared to be his favorite. By then, getting him to nibble some fruit was a little easier, and the warm, soothing shower Jarrod treated him to perked him up a little bit. He treated his welts with ointment, gently spreading some around his hole too. He'd feel it all the way home, that was for certain, but Jarrod was proud of having given his pet everything he'd asked for, especially when it would be several days before he'd be able to take care of him again. He'd slipped the cream in Bastian's bag too, so he wouldn't have to search for some while he was traveling.

Damn, just thinking about the road trips they were each about to undertake had him missing his pet, despite still having him at his side for a little longer.

"Wish we didn't have to go," Bastian murmured as Jarrod slid his sweatpants up his legs and kissed his abs.

"I know, sweetheart. I feel the same way too."

They cuddled for as long as they could, until Jarrod's phone started beeping a fifteen-minute warning at him and it was time to walk through the room one last time and ensure they hadn't forgotten anything.

They'd done good. Everything was packed and ready to be loaded in their vehicles, another sobering thought as he took Bastian's hand, leading him out the door.

Chauncy and Scoundrel were waiting down in the lobby, looking as rumpled as the two of them. No doubt they'd gotten in as much time together as they could manage, especially when a greater distance would separate them when they each got home. Chauncy's eyes looked a little bit puffy, like the kitten had been crying a little, while Scoundrel had shades covering his eyes, making it impossible to see anything but his own reflection staring back at him.

"Was beginning to think you'd decided to extend your stay," Scoundrel said once they'd crossed the room to reach them.

"I thought about it," Jarrod admitted, "but it would be just as hard to leave tomorrow as it's going to be leaving today."

"You can say that again."

Chauncy said nothing, and even Bastian was silent as the four of them carried their bags out into a slightly overcast morning.

"Glad I packed my rain gear," Scoundrel muttered as he cast a look up at the sky.

"You aren't planning on riding in the rain, are you?" Chauncy asked, his voice low and slightly wavering.

"Only as far as I need to, pet," Scoundrel replied, draping an arm over Chauncy's shoulders and giving him a little squeeze. "You don't need to worry about it none. I've been riding for almost as long as you've been alive. I know when it's safe and when to get my ass off the road and I don't take risks when I don't have to. The gear is just to keep me dry in case the rain catches me between exits, which it has a habit of doing."

Judging by the sigh Chauncy let out, Jarrod got the sense that he was relieved to hear that.

"The next time we get together, I'm going to get you on the back of my machine so you can see just how safe she is," Scoundrel said.

"She might be safe, but that doesn't mean the other people on the road with you are," Chauncy said softly, but Jarrod detected a hint of fierceness in his voice, showing a whole new side to Bastian's friend. It was a welcome change, one Jarrod hoped he'd keep developing long after he got home.

"Amen to that. There truly are some knuckleheads out there. They get behind the wheels with their cell phones in one hand and a cup of coffee with the other, trying to steer with their knees while they forget to pay attention to where they're going," Scoundrel griped.

"That's…" Bastian muttered, hands fluttering a bit as he tried to come up with a proper adjective.

"Insane," Chauncy supplied for him. "That didn't seriously happen, did it?"

"That's mild compared to some of the things I've seen," Scoundrel replied. "I once rolled up on an accident where a woman had put her eye out with a mascara wand because she'd been trying to apply the shit while she was driving. Car in front of her stopped short, she slammed into it, the wand slammed into her eye and…"

Chauncy gagged, effectively ending Scoundrel's story.

"Sorry about that, pet."

"It's okay," Chauncy murmured. "Just please no more stories of bloody body parts."

"I'll work on that."

"Thanks."

"No worries," Scoundrel said, giving him a little squeeze. "The last thing I want is to give you nightmares, though I wouldn't be adverse to you calling me in the middle of the night 'cause you couldn't sleep. I'm sure I could think of plenty of ways to turn your fears into something else."

Chauncy's giggles got Bastian to start giggling too, the merry sound lightening the mood, at least until they reached Chauncy's car. It seemed like all too soon the luggage was loaded and the four of them stood around the machine with nothing left to do but say goodbye.

God damn it all, he didn't want to.

"This is even harder than I thought it would be," Jarrod admitted, refusing to loosen his hold on Bastian.

On the other side of the car, Chauncy was in a similar embrace with Scoundrel, Bastian's best friend practically invisible with the way the big medic was wrapped around him. That right there was another event success story, like so many others he'd had the privilege to enjoy this year.

"It'll be okay," Bastian said, though he was cuddled so tight to Jarrod's chest that even if he did let go, Bastian wasn't going anywhere. "In just ten days we'll get to see each other again."

"That's nine days too long."

Bastian giggled at that, a sound Jarrod knew he'd never get tired of hearing. "I promise to video chat as often as possible, especially while we're on the road, that way you can join us at all the cool places we stop to explore."

"I'm looking forward to that."

"I'm really going to miss you," Bastian murmured.

"I'm going to miss you to the moon and back," Jarrod said, stroking that soft, shimmering hair, trying to commit the feel of it to memory.

"Only that far?" Bastian teased, prompting Jarrod to tickle him until he was squirming and trying to get away.

"You're amazing, have I told you that today?" Jarrod asked.

Bastian pouted and comically batted his eyes at him, trying to look hurt, only he couldn't keep the smile off his face. "Nope, you forgot."

"Well, I'm telling you now," Jarrod said. "And I'll tell you every single day, I promise, whether it's over the phone or in person. You will always know how precious you are to me."

"I love you," Bastian said, wrapping his arms around Jarrod's neck and clinging again.

"I love you too, sweetheart, don't you ever doubt that."

"Are you sure you don't want me to come to you next weekend?" Bastian offered for the third time since they'd made their plans.

"Nope, we discussed this remember?" Jarrod said, lightly booping his nose. "I want to see your loft and visit all those amazing places you were telling me about, especially the zip lines. Like I mentioned before, I've never been and I would love for the first time to be with you."

"I…" Bastian stammered, squirming. "It's just….my place is kinda small."

"And it is still your place, and I'm coming, unless you don't want me to."

"No!" Bastian yelped, hugging him again. "That's not what I want at all. I want to see you."

"Then I'll be there, and this is the last time you're going to mention a change of plan, right?"

"Yes, Sir," Bastian replied, nuzzling against the side of Jarrod's neck.

"Good, that's my good boy," Jarrod said stroking his hair. After Chauncy had tipped him off about Claude still sniffing around Bastian, particularly on play nights at the club, Jarrod had decided to make it his mission to meet the man and drop some none-too-subtle hints that Bastian was taken.

Thunder rumbled in the distance, which only served to draw a muttered curse from Scoundrel.

"I–I guess we'd better get going," Chauncy said after Scoundrel opened the car door for him.

"You be good pet," Scoundrel told him, pressing a kiss to his forehead.

"I will. I promise," Chauncy assured him.

"I expect you to be good too," Jarrod told Bastian before finally getting his door open too. "And careful, no more taking on trees."

"I'll do my best to avoid another head on collision with one of them."

"You'd better." Jarrod told him. "I want you in one piece when I see you again, got it."

"Got it."

"Good, now if you start to feel yourself getting sad, or thinking anything has changed between us, just run your fingers over your collar and remember why I put it there, okay?" Jarrod said, kissing him on the tip of his nose again.

"I will."

"And make sure you call when you pull off the road for the night. I want to know that you guys got checked into a hotel safely," Jarrod said.

"That goes for me, too," Scoundrel said.

Both pets nodded. Chauncy even held up the duel phone charger to show it to them before plugging his phone in.

"Where's yours?" Jarrod asked, prompting Bastian to produce it from his back pocket and plug it in beside Chauncy's.

"Good boy," Jarrod said, kissing him one last time before stepping back. "I love you."

"I love you too."

The wince the flashed across Bastian's face when he slid into his seat was a reminder of their morning together, and Jarrod couldn't help but lean over and whisper in his ear. "Is it everything you wanted?"

"Uh-huh," Bastian moaned tipping his face up for another kiss. This one turned hot and heavy in an instant, as images of their bedroom session flashed through Jarrod's head. It was only polite coughing and a hand on his shoulder hauling him back from the car that broke things up.

"You two start doing that and no one is leaving here anytime soon," Scoundrel said, keeping a firm hold on him as Bastian closed the door and Chauncy started up the car, the pair waving and calling out goodbye before finally driving away.

"Ten days," Jarrod muttered. "How the fuck am I going to last that long when I miss him already?"

"You've got a phone, use it. Learn to edge with your voice the same way you do when you've got your hands on him."

"How…" Jarrod muttered.

"Overheard him and Chauncy talking," Scoundrel said, pulling Jarrod into a one-armed hug. "I'd better get moving, get ahead of the rain while I've got the chance. I just hope the cell is slow moving, or I'm going to end up holed up somewhere with shitty internet missing my pet more than I already do."

"You be safe out there."

"You too."

Scoundrel's boots crunched over the stray rocks in the parking lot as he walked away, leaving Jarrod to stare at the empty space where the car had been. There was nothing left now but to seek out his own vehicle and start his own melancholy drive back home. He made it three steps before his phone roared, singling a text coming in.

"I've changed my mind. The moon and back isn't far enough. I want you to love me all the way to Pluto."

All Jarrod could do was stand there and shake his head, laughing at his unpredictable pet. Just like that first moment when he'd caught sight of him flipping and twisting as he tore off along the path, his pet had left him in awe. Fingers flying over the screen, he typed out a message, still chuckling to himself as he did.

"To Pluto and back it is."

Also By Layla Dorine

Guitars and Cages
Guitars and Choices
Desolation Angel
Roadhouse Reds
Broken Prince, Mismatched Eyes
…And All Shall Fade to Black
Serpent's Kiss
Racing the Sky
Midnight Musicals and Coffee Ice Cream
Gemini's Rogue
Tattered Angel
Dust Trail Blues
Bleeding Dawn
Claiming Cody
Burning Luck
Waiting for Raine
Howl Down the Moon
Death Growl
Halfway to Someday
Painted Love
Babber into my Heart
Outlaw Redeemed
Swamp Wolf
A Murder for Crow
Love in Shimmering Chartreuse
A Daddy for Christmas: Ryu
A Little Christmas: Ajay's Secret
Damaged Saints

Milton Keynes UK
Ingram Content Group UK Ltd.
UKHW020632161123
432684UK00016B/599

9 798223 773764